Gauri Deshpande (1942–2003) bilingual poet, essayist and short story writer in Marathi and English, has been published extensively in both languages. Her fluency in them has earned her the reputation of a translator par excellence, one of her most outstanding works being the translation into Marathi of the 16 volumes of Sir Richard Burton's *The Arabian Nights*. The special niche she has carved for herself in the literary world is as a writer who boldly and fearlessly expressed exactly what she felt, always questioning hypocritical societal mores and redefining sexual ethics. Over the years this has often provoked colleagues and critics into remarking that she "writes like a man". Gauri vehemently refutes this saying that, on the contrary, she writes very much like a woman. "In fact, I have understood life and its multiple experiences **because** I am a woman..."

Her collections of poetry include *Between Births* (1968); *Lost Love* (1970); and *Beyond the Slaughterhouse* (1972). Among her prose works are *The Lackadaisical Sweeper* (1997), and the English translation of *Ahe Manohar Tari*.

Deliverance

a novella

Gauri Deshpande

Translated from the original Marathi and with an Afterword by

Shashi Deshpande

984 - 2009 25 YEARS OF FEMINIST PUBLISHING

kali for women

women UNLIMITED

Deliverance: a novella
was first published in English in 2010
by
Women Unlimited
(an associate of Kali for Women)
K-36, Hauz Khas Enclave
New Delhi 110016

ISBN: 81-88965-63-4

Cover design: PealiDezine
Cover painting: Aruna Vasudev

Printed at Raj Press, R-3, Inderpuri, New Delhi 110012
Typeset at Sanchauli Image Composer, B-28, Nawada,
New Delhi 110059

Contents

To Ranju/Janaki/Toshi-Ojisan/Yoshiyo-Hisayo/Dr Abhi

OUR AAI & DADA PASSED AWAY ON NOVEMBER 17, 2012

Mimi-Shami

Dear Mimi,

Your letter gave me such a shock, I wanted to meet you right away; then I remembered that you are not the seventeen or eighteen year old Mimi I first met. You are much older, responsible, capable and dignified. Actually, it is you who should comfort me. Remember when we first got to know each other – years back – what a soggy mess you used to make of my handkerchief? It's because of you that I got to know your Aai and Dada. After your 'recovery' our professional relationship changed into friendship without our realising it. We met less often when they went to live in that way-out place, but their greeting cards and letters which told me what was happening in your and Shami's life, and my meetings with you when you were on your way to visit them – these brought some excitement into my rather dull life. I admired the way all of you faced life with determination and hope; I admit I was proud of it as well. It's not surprising that after living such a rich life, they didn't want to wait for death to slowly creep up on them. This will shock you at first, perhaps even make you angry, but I'm sure you will try to understand, absorb this finally, and then move on.

Will you come to this country as often as before? You must, at least to give some hope to those of us who have been left behind to live out our humdrum lives. I know you will meet me before going back home. Look after each other, there are only the two of you now.

Your
Dr Abhi

— Well, are you Mimi? How are you? Come, sit down. I'm Abhi Raj, your doctor for the next few weeks. Every Wednesday, at 10 o'clock. Is that okay?
— What do I care? Somebody sends me, I come.
— You mean you've come against your wishes?
...
— Tell me, if you don't like me, we'll speak to your mother.
— It's not that. I have to listen to *someone's* lecture, better you than that third-rate college. At least you're better looking than my Sir.
— Thanks. But I'm not going to lecture you, you're going to be talking to me.
— I have nothing to say to you. What's there to say? And what will you understand?
— Nothing at all? That's good! That's excellent. Let's just sit and stare at each other then. I've never earned my fees so easily before.
— How did she ever think that I would speak to you?
— You don't want to talk to her, or to your mama and mavshi, you won't talk to any of her friends either, so she thought you might speak more freely to a stranger.
— Correct. She'd have a fit if she heard any of these things!
— What things?
— I mean – about my own father behaving improperly with me.
— With you?
— What do you mean 'with you?' Did you hear what I said, Doctor? I love him. L-O-V-E. And you know who the man is? My father. F-A-T-H-E-R.
— Not really your FATHER.
— Okay then, my mother's husband. What difference does it make?
— If you think it does, it does.
— No difference at all. Taboo, huh? Listen to this now. He

loves me, too. L-O-V-E. Are you shocked? Or are psychiatrists never shocked?

— Of course they are. But not by small things.

— Small? A daughter loving her father is a small thing?

— All girls love their fathers and all boys love their mothers. So what? I, too, am in love with my mother.

— Don't try to provoke me by acting the innocent, you think I was born yesterday? You want me to spell it out? My father … he … with me … I mean, well, I wanted him to screw me.

— Really?

— Still not shocked? When I told my friend he was horrified!

— Then we have to accept that my shock threshold is a little higher than your friend's, don't we?

— And my father had the same thing in mind. What do you say now?

— You're a young, healthy, pretty girl. If you kept trying to fall into my arms all day, I'd probably feel the same!

— (*Laughing*) Really? You'd have felt that?

— But that doesn't mean I would have done anything about it.

— Huh. (*Grumbling*) He didn't do anything, either. (*Quickly*) But I hugged and kissed him. He was scared, I know that. And he didn't tell *her* about it.

— How do you know?

— I know. If he had, she'd have packed my bags immediately and sent to me to Father – my real father, I mean.

— Would that have been okay by you?

— No! I don't like my mother very much, but she's better than that bitch my father married. She's like a snapping dog. What's the matter – don't like my language?

— If that's how you feel, that's the kind of language you need. But don't say it to your father – your real father – or you might get slapped.

— Ha! He slap me! Even my mother has never slapped me.

— Is that why you don't like her?

— What? What do you mean?
— I think she should have smacked you now and then, it would have been good for both of you.
— But she never hit me, it didn't matter what I did. She would just stop speaking to me. Nothing ever got to her, nothing. She put on a good act when she was among people, mother and daughter facing the world together, and so on. But between us – a locked door. Knock on it as much as you like, but nothing. Some of her friends tried to speak to her on my behalf – no use. One thing I must say, they are very good to me. Even when I was little they did exactly what I wanted. What have you to say to that?
— Everybody is kind to a little girl.
— But *she* wasn't, she wasn't.

. . .

— There, you see! You've fallen for her, too.
— Fallen? I've only met her once.
— Listen, she can win over a person in three minutes. As far as that goes I have to hand it to her – she's absolutely the best.
— Is that why you dislike her?
— Hah! If you had everyone praising your mother all your life, you would understand. 'You're her daughter, are you? I'd never have guessed.' Why not? Why wouldn't you have guessed? Because I'm a fool? Almost an idiot? Is that what she told you? 'Will you help my mentally deficient daughter?' (*Begins crying.*)
— (*Lightly*) No, no. She only said my daughter badly needs your help. Something is hurting her and I don't know how to help.
— (*Sobbing loudly*) But I like my mother, truly. She's my mother. I love her, I *do*.
— Of course you do. Did I say you don't? Here, take this hanky. Come on, that's better. Now come next week, okay?

— Doctor, who was that peculiar looking man, the one who just went out?
— Why do you ask?
— Ha! You don't have to be a doctor all the time! Tell me, who was he? He looked like an idiot.
— He may well have said the same thing about you.
— Never! He would have said, 'Now who is this beautiful girl?' Do you think I'm beautiful? Tell me, do you? You do, don't you? *Tell me.*
— You're okay.
— Damn!
— (*Laughing*) There's still time, you'll soon be a beauty. Okay?
— So you think *she's* beautiful.
— Who?
— She. *She.* Who else? Everyone says, 'Your mother is so beautiful.' You just don't want to admit it.
— Mimi! I've only met her once, and at the time both of us were thinking only of you.
— Were you? Thinking of me, were you? Ha! Did you hold her hand – the poor thing – to comfort her, or did you wipe her eyes? Hanh? What did you do? Tell me! Why don't you speak now? Did you hold her hand? Wipe her tears?
— No. She sat in the chair you're sitting on and asked me to help you. Her hands were around her bag and my hands were on the table, the way you see them now. She wasn't crying. She was sad, but she didn't seem to be confused or frightened. Very calmly she asked me to help you. Okay?
— No! It's not okay! What else did she say? (*Imitating*) 'That idiotic disgusting girl wants to take MY husband away. We have to do something about her.' Or, 'We must put that mad girl into a hospital. Won't you help me?'
— She didn't say anything like that.
— No? Then what? (*Imitating again*) 'Doctor, please, please …' or did she call you Abhi right away? ' …won't you help my

poor, young, good and beautiful daughter? I can't bear to see the way she's ruining her life and ours as well.' She plays that role very well. But shall I tell you the truth? She's jealous of me because I'm young, good and pretty.

— Really? Is that what you think?

— Yes, really. That's what I think.

— It's possible. We do envy a lot of people, nothing unusual about that.

— What? Not even about mothers being jealous of their daughters?

— Not very.

— Then there's nothing unusual about daughters being jealous of their mothers, either.

— No, there isn't.

— What about daughters despising their mothers? Surely that's unusual?

Do you despise yours?

— *Yes.* Contempt, anger spite, envy …

— Why?

— Why not? When has she done me any good? I was her doll, wasn't I? Her cute little doll. She even used to call me that, to prove that she was different from the others, that she was superior. Most women, when they give birth they suffer pain, they are surrounded by caring people, but not her – she gave birth just like that! She always said that she had absolutely no trouble at all. (*As she speaks, she begins to imitate*) I never cried or whined or fell ill or had tantrums. Nothing! As if I was a lump of clay and had a good shape only because of her. As if I was the cakes and bread she makes which everyone keeps praising!

— But isn't there some truth in all this?

— No! Not at all! Not a bit. I am me. Understand? ME. That's what he saw and that's why he fell in love with me. And that's why she's jealous! She's going to lock me up, isn't she? In a hospital? With your help?

— Mimi, Mimi! I'm going to help you. It's my job to help you. You're the most important person here, do you understand?
— Really?
— Yes, really. Isn't that why your mother sent you to me?
— No! She never thinks I'm important. Her one aim is to get rid of this nuisance somehow. Once you've washed out my brain, she'll fold me up and put me inside a drawer – like before. Didn't she say so to you?
— No.
— There! Now she's taken you in. She does that to everyone. She says all kinds of things about me, she's told him lots of things against me, too. He doesn't talk to me any more, doesn't even look at me. When I enter a room he leaves. And she, too, she doesn't meet my eyes now. They don't even look at each other. (*Laughs loudly*) Breakfast at home is such a sight! Nobody looks at anyone, nobody talks, everyone looks out of the window or at the wall or the newspaper. There's absolute silence. (*Cries*) Only Shami speaks to me. She comes to me and says, 'Mimi, Mimi ...' I like Shami a lot, I like her very, very, very much. A *lot*. (*Sobs loudly*)
— Tch, tch. Here, take this hanky. And next week bring your own, okay? Now blow your nose. That's it. Good. See? I can comfort a person without holding hands.
— I'll come next week.

— Hi. How are you?
— (*Laughing*) Fine. And you? New salwar-kameez, I see. Looks lovely.
— We'd gone to buy Shami a frock and we saw this. I liked it so much that Aai bought it for me. Shami wanted something just like this but Aai said, Cchi! That's the 'we two sisters' style.
— How old is your Shami?

— Five. She's sweet, she's my pet. Because of her I stopped being alone, I had company.
— Mimi and Shami – don't the names match?
— No. Our names are not alike. But can a child of one-and-a-half say 'Amrita'? Aai tried hard to teach her 'Amritadidi', and this brat would say 'Mimi'. And that stuck. Her name is Shalmali. Obviously that became Shami.
— It's fun having a younger sister, isn't it?
— Yes, great fun. The way she keeps meddling in everything, Aai and I laugh at her all day. Then she becomes weepy and says, 'Don't laugh at Shami', and we laugh all the more. But *he* doesn't like me to laugh at her, says she'll get some kind of complex. Which means work for you all over again.
— Thanks, I don't want that kind of work. Does she go to school?
— Of course! She's clever. She already reads and writes both Marathi and English. I couldn't do that!
— You remember that, do you?
— No. Dada – he – says so. I was seven when I first met him. I was stupid.
— Does he say that?
— (*Suddenly angry*) No, he doesn't, *I* say it. He says I was so sweet, so good. I knew my eight times table, I sang English songs …
— So you were clever!
— But I told him, 'Go away, I don't like you.' He must have said something nice to me because I was a little girl. But I said, very sharply, 'I don't want your flattery. My mother and I are getting on very well without you.' And he would reply, 'Come on,' just like you. He said, 'If you say your eight times table, I'll teach you to make a mouse with a handkerchief.' And I said – (*voice gradually gets quavery, finally stops*) I said, 'I know how to, Ajoba taught me.' I behaved so badly with him. Right from the start. But he never took it seriously.

…

— (*Blowing her nose*) He even used to give me a bath and comb my hair – like he does with Shami now. But he says – he said once – my hair was thicker and I didn't cry as much as she does. Ha! That brat! How she howls! Day and night, she goes wah wah for the smallest thing. Even Aai gets fed up. But Dada – he picks her up immediately. 'No, no, good baby. Don't cry, Dada is here.' Aai gets furious. She says, 'No need to pet her so much,' but he replies, 'Come on, what's wrong with petting a little girl?' She's a great pet of his. His only child. It goes on all the time. Give her this, give her that, play cards with her, teach her games – I get so bored. What can you talk about with that silly fool? But he can! They go on for hours. When she comes home the first thing is, 'What did our Chami do in school today?' What does she do in school? The same thing over and over again. ABC, ABC. But she starts her, 'Dada, Dada' and tells him a lo-o-o-ng story. And he listens. Wholeheartedly. If I try to interrupt and speak about my college, the stupid creature starts howling. Then my Aaisaheb packs me off to my room. Anything for a bit of peace and quiet. I go to my room, put on some music and have a smoke. Well, aren't you shocked?
— At what?
— At my smoking?
— No, I smoke too, sometimes. But honestly, it isn't good for your health. Does your mother know?
— She knows. And what did she say? (*Imitating*) 'Now you're eighteen, old enough to know what's good for you. But it's a bad habit. It'll be good if you give it up.'
— I must say your mother is very liberal. Actually she should have forbidden your smoking.
— As if I would have listened!
— Maybe that's why she didn't, she knew it was no use.
— What do you think? But Dada – he – told her, 'She can't smoke in the house.' And she said, 'What's the use? It'll only mean more concealment, more lies.' I heard them. And he

said, 'Then tell her if she wants to smoke she can go to her room and smoke. The air in this house belongs to all of us, she has no right to pollute it.' And Aai said, 'Tell her yourself.'
— Did he?
— (*Softly*) Yes, he did.
— And you obeyed him?
— Yes. Everyone obeys him. When he speaks sternly, even Shami listens to him. If she's howling, he only has to say, 'That's enough,' for her to stop at once. He doesn't say much, but when he does, you have to listen. I used to obey him even when I was little. But *she* told him, 'This girl is my responsibility, I'm going to deal with her.' As if I was a heavy burden! We used to have fun, Dada and I. I would ask him, 'When will I get a nice plump chest?' And he would get out a tape and measure me and write in the diary: 22-22-22. And sometimes Aai would say, 'You can't include measurements of the back in that!' So she would get the tape, measure me, and write: a quarter inch higher than the armpit. It was such fun, the three of us had such fun! Then they both left me and went away and had their own daughter – this creature. It's no fun for her, I can tell you. I'm always shouting, Aai yells at her, and he just looks at her and goes out. Sometimes I feel sorry for Shami and take her out for an ice-cream. You must come and see our house. Either everyone is shouting, or else it's as quiet as a grave. You know why? You know, don't you? It's because of me.
— Do you enjoy it then?
— Yes, I do. Of course I do. They're hopeless, this is what they deserve. Very few people visit us now. God knows what they've told everyone, but the truth is that people simply don't visit us. As if we've got the plague or cholera. So now there's the silence of the grave. Serious faces. Like we're in mourning.
— And earlier?
— It used to be fun! We had such fun. Sometimes we had fights, there was shouting and screaming, but on the whole it

was wonderful. Before *he* came, she and I had a great time. She would take me everywhere. Everyone made such a fuss over me. She didn't have much money – we either went second class or we walked. Even at night. But I was never scared, Aai was with me, wasn't she? She had warned me – if anyone acts funny, just yell loudly. Once a man shoved me – the way she set upon him! Just one look at her face and he ran away! And we laughed and laughed at his fright. Sometimes we used to go out and eat bhel, Saturdays and Sundays. There wasn't enough money to eat in a restaurant, but we still enjoyed ourselves. Sometimes her friends came with us but most of them were poor as well. If someone had money, we indulged ourselves – ice-cream and a taxi. After Dada married Aai things were a little better. Not that Dada had much money, but with both of them working it was okay. He had an old Fiat – we named it the chariot of Jagannath, you had to either pull it or push it. God knows where it is now. They got rid of it before going … (*Silent for a while*)

— And where did you go on your holidays?

— (*With some enthusiasm*) To my Ajoba. He had a big house and garden, a dog, a cat, a car and chauffeur, a cook – great! The moment he saw us, Ajoba would begin scolding Aai: 'What is this! You don't look after the child, she's all bones. Now Amrita, Francis will cook whatever you want. Chicken curry and baked fish and custard pudding. Just you see how plump we'll make you in a month!' I remember Ajji too. Actually, she died when I was young. She would teach me to recite shlokas, she would peel the grapefruit, sprinkle sugar on it and give it to me. She would make rava laddus. Oh, I was so petted and spoilt. And there were my cousins, Viru and Biju, at Mavshi's. They used to pamper me as well. I had a great time when I was little, much more than others. Other mothers only cooked and scolded and told their children not to talk to us. And their fathers! Paunchy old men. When they saw Aai and Dada, they would look the other way. But we had such fun. (*Begins to cry*) The two of us, we had great fun, and so did the three of us. Then, because I was grown up, they packed me off to a school. And they left, went far away and he had his own brat. Why will he talk to me now? He doesn't even look at me. Doesn't look, doesn't listen. Doctor, please tell him to talk to me. Tell him I won't do it again. I like him a lot, I like Dada very much. I like Dada's Shami – I mean, my Shami – very much. Isn't she my little sister? Who else do I have? Who else talks to me? Who else comes into my room?

— There you go again! Have you brought your hanky? No? So it's mine again. Bring them all back, will you? Better if you wash them first. Come. We'll meet next week.

— I've brought her up since she was seven. I won't say I did it as if she was my own child, because actually I loved her more than Shami. Why should she turn against me like this? And in this way? Such filthy accusations!

— But you're assuming that she's clever, that she understands and has done this knowingly. That's where you're wrong.

— But doesn't she? She's eighteen, she must understand.

— She doesn't want to be eighteen, she thinks she lost all her fun and enjoyment when she 'grew up'.

— She talks and you listen. Ask her how much she's still spoilt and indulged. She has her own room, a hundred rupees pocket money, and all the clothes, jewellery, make-up, books and records she wants. And heaps of boyfriends. Nobody ever says do this or why haven't you done that. But as far as studies go, a big zero. What do you mean, no more fun? It's been fun all her life! Her mother indulged her because she didn't have a father, and I did the same. And my reward? This!

— Maybe she thinks you're trying to get rid of her by giving

her all these things.
— So what do I do then? Take them all away from her? Punish her and force her to study?
— It's natural for you to be angry, I was only trying to remind you that emotionally, she's still a child. She needs your love and your time – not things.
— Great! And we're regretting the fact that we've given her too much love and time! We should have sent her to a hostel or to her father when I married her mother. But I thought, no! This is a challenge, I will think of this girl as my own. And now? I'm disgraced among our friends.
— Why do you say that? Your friends will believe you, not a confused girl of eighteen.
— Our friends may not believe it, but the story is bound to spread. It'll soon reach strangers and then our colleagues, hers and mine.
— You're strong enough to face that, but this girl is not – don't forget that. The two of you have to support her now, you can't turn your backs on her.

...

— She has a lot of regard for you. Yes, she does. It's not surprising that she should have such fantasies. But these fantasies have frightened her. That such thoughts should come into her mind has bewildered her. How can she ask for help? And from whom? Just imagine – what if she had spoken to her mother?
— (*Abashed*) Her mother is quick to anger, she'd have cut her off at once.
— That's what she was afraid of. You had left her once and gone away, that caused her enough anguish. And – let me be frank – she's jealous of your daughter. She's yours, and Mimi was afraid that because of her, you would neglect her.
— Jealous? Listen, she's always standing up for that child, she's spoilt her. Shami is constantly in her sister's room, doesn't listen to her parents. In fact the two of them have made us outsiders.

— This is also because of her fear. If there's no one else at least her sister is hers – that's the way she thinks. She also thinks that if she keeps reminding herself that Shami is her younger sister, she can control her own wild thoughts.

— But that hasn't happened. She went and told her boyfriend all kinds of stuff. And because it's such an enormous thing, his parents told her mother. How do we unravel this tangle now? It has to stop.

— Don't say that. Don't you feel for her at all?

— (*In sudden excitement*) Doctor, how do I tell you? I thought of her as my daughter, we never imagined we would have this younger one. We were in a foreign country and her mother cried day and night because she was missing her daughter. It's because she insisted that we had this child. I still think of the older girl as more my own. When she cried and had tantrums, it was I who fed her, not her mother. When she woke up sobbing at night, she said 'Dada' first, not 'Aai'. I've given ten years of my life to her, to this family – to building our family.

— And will you now destroy it because of a young girl's blunder?

— Blunder? This? It's a crime!

— No, it's just a blunder. She was desperate, she didn't know what to do, she was frightened and confused. But this too came from love. She was pulled in different directions by her love for three people, and it must have driven her to behaving so oddly. Even in ordinary families there are pressures which can make a person snap. And yours …

— But everything was going so well until now …

— Think of this. She went to a hostel when she was thirteen, and then you left for a new place on transfer and had a child immediately. What was she to think? That you got rid of her and were starting afresh.

— But, Doctor, she enjoyed the little one so much! It's true. And the child prefers Mimi to her parents.

— Therefore the conflict. On the one hand there's love – she loves her sister dearly – and on the other, there are bad feelings because she's your 'real' daughter. The same goes for you.
— For me?
— Why not? You brought stability, security and a father's love into her life, so she loves you. But you came between her and her mother, so she's angry. Try to remember – wasn't she resentful of you at first?
— Yes, but she loved me just as much. (*Laughing*) I remember once when I had gone to Dehradun, she was reading *The Maneaters of Kumaon* and she thought a tiger would get me! She created such a furore all night. (*In a trembling voice*) I loved her very much, too.
— It's not just love that people have for one another. Just as your love now has a veil of anger, her earlier anger was a facade for love. Anger is bound to show through love and love through anger. Doesn't she get angry with the very sister she loves so much – because she shares your love?
— Then, for the same reason, she must be angry with her mother as well.
— Of course.
— What?
— She's furious with her mother – for many different reasons.
— What are you saying? She and her mother are … like this! Like Siamese twins.
— But won't a growing girl get impatient with such emotional dependence? She's been competing with her mother for a long time. As you say they were more – well, Siamese twins than mother and daughter, and now this tangle. She's confronting her mother with her mother's own weapons. Do you understand?
— A bit. It's too complicated.
— The human mind is very complicated.
— That's why you're needed.
— We don't understand much ourselves. Only one thing: that

most things can be solved through love and affection. Certainly between parents and children.

— (*Softly*) Are they really solved? But (*loudly*) I'm no saint. How can I not think of all these things when I'm talking to her or dealing with her? Earlier, she used to give me a kiss before going to bed, would hug me when I came home from a trip. It was done so easily. And I would also hold her close without thinking about it. How can we do that now? Every word, every action, is coloured by her accusations …

— Please try. I admit it's hard but you must not turn away from her. It's a question of four or five years only. If a person's – no, your own daughter's – entire life and happiness depend on it, shouldn't you do this much?

— I have to, don't I? Who else can do it? Thank you, Doctor.

— Thank you. And goodbye.

— I'm likely to be transferred again.

— When? And where do we go?

— In four or five months. To Japan.

— So what do we do?

— We go.

— And Mimi's college? Shami's fine, she's just started school, she can go to school there as well. But Mimi?

— You know, I think it's better for me to be away from Mimi for a while. I was going to tell Abhi Raj one of these days that I'm finding this very difficult. And because of all these peculiar happenings, Shami is being pushed around. You, too.

— Yaju, you didn't ask for this transfer, did you?

— Not exactly, but …

— When the question arose of who should go, you jumped at it.

— Yes.

— Go, then.
— And you?
— We'll manage.
— Don't be like this. Must I live alone for two years? Shami won't recognise me when I come back.
— And Mimi? I can't just forget about her – like you!
— What about a hostel ...?
— Wasn't one experience enough? What will she think – these two just get rid of me, put me in a hostel or keep me at home according to their convenience? Abhi Raj said a lot of this came out when she was with him. Actually, she's quite tough but does that mean we push her to the limit?
— Where will you stay?
— We can stay here for six months, then it'll be the summer vacations. After that, we'll try for paying guest accommodation – something like that.
— She'll complete her B.A in a year and a half. Will you come after that, at least? Think about it. A new country, a completely different culture, new experiences, new friends – you'll feel better.
— You think so, Yaju? How did things get so out of hand? Sometimes even Shami behaves so oddly. I wonder whether I'm going mad.
— She's only a child, and all this tension is bound to affect her as well. However much we protect them, children sense the atmosphere around them. Everything will be fine when you come there. So – decided?
— Only after Mimi completes her B.A and proper arrangements are made for her further studies, or a job – or whatever.
— Please say yes. At least prepare yourself for happiness! She'll be grown up by then.
— Yes.
— I'll be able to come here after a year. Decide by then, so that I can look out for a house and prepare for your arrival.

— Look, don't nag me. I'll tell you in a year. What's the hurry? Let's leave it for the time being.

— Shami, look, new-new blue toothpaste! Open your mouth, let me brush.
— I want to brush, I want to brush.
— Let me brush first, then you can.
— No, I'm going to brush first.
— All right. But move aside and let me rinse out my mouth, I have to make the tea. You can brush after that.
— No, me first, me first.
— Okay, brush, but be quick.
...
— Haven't you finished yet? My God! You've chewed up the brush, it's ruined. Do I have to get you a new toothbrush every day? What's wrong with you?
— Waah! Take your toothbrush, I won't brush my teeth. Won't brush, won't brush.
— All right, don't brush. Your teeth will rot and fall out. What do I care?
— Yours will also fall out.
— Why will they?
— Because you're an old woman.

— Aai, Aai, Aai! (*Banging on the door*) *Aaaaaiii!*
— What are you doing? Aai has gone to the toilet.
— I want Aai. *Aaaii!*
— Shami, stop this nonsense! Tell me what you want, I'll give it to you.
— I want Aai! (*Bangs on the door*)

— What is it? What do you want? Can't I even go to the toilet in the morning?
— I want you. What are you doing?
— I'm sleeping, okay? Take her away, Mimi.
— She won't listen to me!
— Show her something interesting then.
— Shami, come here, baby. Drink your milk. And look, there's a picture of a plane in the paper.
— *Aaaa.* I want Aai. *Aaa ...ii!*
(Loud sound of door opening.)
— Here! Here's Aai. Take her! From now on, I'll wake up at four in the morning and get it over with. Why do we need this tamasha at the bathroom door every morning? You wanted Aai, didn't you? Here I am! What do you want me to do? Sit by you all day?
— Show me the plane in the paper.

Dear Janaki,

Mimi has completed her B.A. She was never interested in it, so I had to work harder for Mimi's B.A. than I did for my own. She absolutely refuses to go for further studies. One good thing is that, since she's such an active and curious person, she has many interests and knows people from various professions. One of them has offered her a job. He's a photographer. She has to look after the studio and equipment and help the models who work for him. In return she will get some money, a tiny room next to the studio to live in and a bit of professional training. I am very reluctant to say yes. The fact is, though Mimi seems grown up, she's barely twenty. The second thing is, how can we trust that man? (Though he seems okay and none of the people we asked had anything to say against him.) And, thirdly, the room he has given her is the size of a cabin. She's going to have a tough time living in it. But Mimi is wildly excited because she can live independently as well as work and earn money. Besides, she likes photography. One of her pictures even got a prize from an amateur photographers' society. When I think of all this I want to say 'yes'. Anyway, I don't think she'll listen to me if I say 'no'. Besides, Yaju is waiting for me over there. I will have to leave Mimi 'to her fate' (as Ranju says) sooner or later. But should it be now? Next Saturday I will leave the two girls by themselves and come to you for two days and talk to my heart's content. Is that okay? Last time you were involved with Madhu's going to Calcutta, we couldn't talk much. Do you have time now?

Honestly, I'm surprised that in spite of having an uncomplicated son like Madhu, you understand the problems of my wayward daughter so well. Surprised also that while both of us have had difficult experiences, your Madhu has not been affected by them whereas my daughter has. Actually, our views – yours and mine – are very alike; our natures and experiences as well. But perhaps, as you once said, boys don't take things so much to heart. Besides, you don't consider it humiliating to ask anyone for help which is why, even after Sharu went out of your life, you had your parents, brothers and sisters, uncles and aunts. Why, even your former sisters-in-law and mother-in-law still visit you! So, it was never just Madhu and you; none of us felt that your life was empty in any way. After Ravi and I separated, Mimi and I were on our own for years, just the two of us. Now we are two into two and our problems have also multiplied, not twice but ten times over. Well, let's leave that. I'll chatter to my heart's content when I come there.

— Wake up, wake up. The alarm has already gone off.
— Umm…?
— Come on, be quick! Otherwise you'll end up rushing around and crying like you do every day.
— Five minutes more.
— No way. It's already five minutes since the alarm went off.
— Five more, only five.

— Come *on*, get up. Must we go through this nonsense every day? I said, *get up*. Up. (*Pulls the blanket*) Start moving.
— (*Stamps out, door bangs.*)
— Cocoa, cocoa, where's my cocoa?
— Here, right in front of you.
— It's so cold, heat it up.
. . .
— Tch. Now it's too hot. How can I drink it?
— Your eyes are still gooey. Wash them and comb your hair, it'll cool down by then.
— No. Then it'll be too cold and you won't heat it up again.
— Come on, drink it up. It's cool enough now.
— But it's got skin on top. Strain it.
— Here, take this. Drink it and go for your bath. You're getting late.
— But it isn't sweet, I want more sugar.
— You shouldn't have so much sugar. Hasn't the dentist told you that?
— Then I don't want it.
— If you don't want it, throw it out. Just go and have a bath quickly.
— What's the time?
— Eight.
— There's no time for my bath then. I'll have it when I come home.
— You say this every day. In the evening, you play, then have dinner, do your studies and fall asleep watching TV. When will you bathe? Go now. Quickly.

(*Sound of door banging*)

. . .
— Aren't you done? How long will you take?
— You're the one who tells me: wash this, clean that – eyes and ears, bum and mouth …
— Okay, okay, that's enough. Stop wasting water.

— Towel – where's the towel?
— Why do you forget it every day? Here. And mind, I won't do this tomorrow.
— Where's my uniform?
— Where did you leave it last evening? Here it is, lying on the floor. How often do I have to tell you to put it on a hanger?
— It's so crumpled. Why don't you iron it?
— If you throw it on the ground, it's going to be crumpled. If you don't care about it, why should I iron it? Wear it as it is.
— Teacher will scold me.
— Let her. Maybe then you'll hang it up neatly on a hanger.

(*Grumbling. Things being thrown around.*)

— And socks? There's not a single pair here.
— Must be in the drawer.
— Where?
— My God! Is this a room or a pigsty? How will you ever find anything? (*Drawers being opened*) The socks are here.
— But they're not a pair.
— Damn it! There's only a small difference in the design, who's going to notice? They're white, aren't they? Wear them. Quickly! You're getting late.

(*Voice: Shami, Shami! It's nine o'clock*)

— There's Angela calling you.
— I still have to pack my bag.
— My God! Be quick. What do you have today? Drawing? Where's your sketch book?
— On the table.
— How can you find anything in this mess? And where's the pencil? Why don't you pack your bag at night?
— Why don't you remind me?

(*Voice: Shami, Shami, come on! Otherwise I'm going.*)

— Shami! Don't forget your lunch box. Have you taken it?

(*Door bangs. Running footsteps.*)

(*From a slight distance*) Come back and take your box! And don't run. Be careful.

(*An irritated weepy voice*) Why don't you wake me up early? Every day the same rushing around.

(*Door bangs again*)

...

— Hi, I'm home. Aha! What are mother and daughter doing at the table? Already having your dinner?
— She won't drink her cocoa, she won't drink her milk and she won't eat her sandwich.
— I didn't say anything about the sandwich, Dada. It's she who won't let me eat it.
— Why don't you drink your cocoa?
— It's not sweet.
— Then add some sugar.
— The dentist will get angry.
— Give her some sugar today, I'll reason with her later. Come on. Why are both of you so stubborn? She's just a child, can't you give in to her a bit?
— I'm always giving in. To both these girls. Here, take it! Take ten spoons if you want. What do I lose? But promise me that if your teeth fall out when you grow up, you won't blame your mother. After all, I'm here to take the blame for everything that goes wrong. If something good happens, it's because of you, but if something goes wrong, your mother becomes the scapegoat!
— Just one extra spoon of sugar – aren't you going too far?
— Yes, stand up for her. And in her presence, so she'll be even more willing to obey me. This goes on from morning to night. Come on, come on, get up! Brush your teeth. Drink your cocoa. Have your bath. Comb your hair. Wear your uniform.

Pack your bag. Don't forget your lunch. Come in. Have a wash. Eat your sandwich. Finish your studies before you go out to play. Or, come home in time. So late! Now, when will you eat and when will you study? Go on, go to bed. My God! I tell you, I'm fed up of hearing my own voice … When will this end? Will it ever end? Is there nothing else to be said all day?
— Shami! Go out and play.
— It's too late now. Who's there to play with?
— Then go to your room. Study. Read a book or watch TV. Go on. (*Stamping of feet.*) Shami! Go quietly and don't bang the door.
— Why have you taken things to such an extreme today?
— The last two years, it's been the same, the same thing every single day. Today I'm exhausted and fed up – that's all.
— She'll grow up in another two years, improve on her own.
— You said the same thing two years ago.
— But what's the difference between six and eight?
— Then what's the difference between eight and ten or between ten and twelve? What difference will it make? Finally, I'll just stop speaking because I'm tired of these endless arguments.
— Look, if you can't be patient with a girl of eight …
— Patient? Patient? Isn't there a limit to patience? You can say a thing gently once, ten times, a hundred times; but after that? Why don't you try it once? Let me take a holiday and you handle her yourself every day.
— How do other mothers manage to bring up children? How did your mother cope? Mine …?
— If you wanted 'other mothers' why did you want me to have this child?
— That's not fair. It was you who wanted this child, not I. If you don't want her now …
— Then what? *What?* (*Voice cracks*) I must have been crazy, I should have learnt a lesson from the first one. What an idiot I am, a moron. The biggest fool. And useless as well. See if you

can find some 'other mother' to bring her up. And go away, both of you!
— Now you've really gone mad, talking such nonsense, putting an end to fifteen years of living together …
— Fifteen or twenty years, what difference does it make? If there's going to be a constant simmering like this – I've had enough.
— This seems to be a case of murder being easier the second time around.
— (*Almost screeching*) *Yaju!*
— My God! I'm sorry! What have I said? I am sorry, sorry. Forgive me. I was angry and spoke rashly. How could I have said that? Please! Oh, God!
— (*Openly sobbing*)You said it because you were thinking it.
— But one doesn't need to utter all one's thoughts!
— Better to do that! How long has this thought been with you? It sounded so rehearsed.

Oh, God! Please! I didn't mean it. Honestly. I was only thinking about finding some way to end your arguments …. Why don't you take someone's help?
— So, it's all my fault. Go on.
— She's just a little girl.
— Little! *Little!* So how does she know exactly what enrages her mother? And after she's done that, she sits back and laughs at my torment. Now that she's made us quarrel, she'll be sitting in her room and laughing!
— What are you saying? Children are devastated by their parents' fights.
— Not this one! Go to her room and see. She'll ask you to sit down and chat with her.
— Rubbish!
— Go and see for yourself. She tries to provoke me very deliberately. And when I lose my temper, she has good reason to carry tales and get you on her side.

— My God! Your imagination is running wild. She's only eight years old!

— Yaju, tell me something. Honestly. Do you remember if we ever fought over anything, even once, before this girl arrived?

...

— Tell me! Mimi created such a terrible situation for us but we faced it together. Sometimes I defended her, sometimes you did. But do you ever remember a confrontation like this, when it was me against you and the child? How is it that she does exactly the kind of things that enrage me?

— All children do things that annoy their parents.

— No, they don't. They have their own preoccupations. She has no occupation apart from driving her mother to the edge. The moment I have a book in my hand, she wants her cocoa or something to eat. She calls me fat at least once a day, tells me I'm an old woman, calls me greedy. Every day she throws her wet towel on her bed, leaves her lunch box in her bag so that it stinks ...

— Come on, all kids ...

— *No*, not all. Do you ever remember doing such things? We got ready quietly and went to school. Did our mothers have to scream at us? How is it that her towel is always on her bed? If it's just carelessness why isn't it on the floor or on the back of the chair sometimes?

— Why don't you tell her instead of making an issue of it?

— Every day?

— Yes, every day.

— Then I become quarrelsome and shrill, I get into the habit of nagging.

— In which case, pick up the towel yourself.

— Every day?

— Yes, every day.

— But why? Is it something an eight year old girl can't do?

— Let her bed get damp.

— When she goes to bed at night she complains, 'My bed is wet, I'll sleep on your bed.'
— Force her to sleep on the damp bed.
— Then I'll have to deal with her colds and coughs! When she gets cavities because she eats sugar, I'm the one who has to take her to the dentist. If I let her off having a bath because of the fuss she makes, she gets heat boils and skin infections and I'm the cause. Others eat and praise my cooking, but she doesn't like it and so every single day it's a cheese sandwich. And I'm to blame for her vitamin deficiency ...
— For God's sake! Take that stone and bash me on the head with it.
— Yaju, is that a solution?
— What should I do then? You tell me.
— I don't know. Try and talk to her and see if she listens. Why don't you try to see my point? All you see is my big mouth.
— But aren't you exagger ....
— Enough! It's over. I won't say anything to her now.
— Don't do that. How will she know what's right or wrong unless her mother tells her?
— Does she understand when she's told? If I tell her, I'm in the wrong and if I don't, I'm still wrong. Better to remain silent and save my energy – I can use it elsewhere.
— Okay. I'll talk to her.

— Listen, should we go to Kamakura tomorrow to see the cherry blossoms?
— But it's Saturday, Shami has a holiday.
— Of course.
— The two of you go, I saw it last year.
— Come on! You don't want to do anything these days, you just sit at home and watch TV or go for walks by yourself.

— What else can I do?
— Come to Kamakura tomorrow.
— No. There will be bitterness and the whole day will be ruined. You go to Kamakura, I'll go to the gardens in Tokyo or to Kita-no-maru. The main thing is to see the cherry blossoms, why do we need company for that?
— Please, why are you doing this?
— Yaju, it'll begin the moment we set out. *Wear your overcoat.* I feel hot. *Okay, your sweater at least.* No. Then, after we set out, half a mile later she'll feel cold. Then she'll be scared of the crowds, then she'll be thirsty, then hungry, then she'll start pestering us with, 'How much longer?' and when we get there it will be, 'When are we going back?' There will be no pleasure either in the flowers or in being together. You and she get on, you take her. If you don't want that, leave her here and go by yourself and I'll see it on Monday before she returns from school. Okay?
— Never mind. Forget it.

Dear Ranju,

Mimi's letter arrived today, and for a moment I wondered what and who she was talking about. I've excised the man called her father so completely from my life that I had forgotten he's alive and living happily in some part of the world. He wrote to Mimi on her 21st birthday, inviting her to visit him. He chose the right time to write – my consent is no longer needed. If she had decided to go it would have been futile to try and make her change her mind. But the tone of her letter suggests that she is wavering. There are two schools of thought in our family. Tai says, don't send her, absolutely not! (Janaki's opinion seems to be the same, but it's not as strong.) Basically, Tai never liked Ravi and the scandal created by our separation turned her dislike to hatred. She thinks it's better not to send Mimi to a man like him. But Yaju says, let her go. In any case, she's just wasting her life in Mumbai doing a useless job. Maybe when she's there she'll be inspired to find a new direction or to use her knowledge more purposefully. If you ask me I, too, think she should go. At this age her father's influence won't harm her. And, as Yaju says, there's a greater possibility that a new direction will do her good. The problem is this: if I tell her that she can certainly go, won't she think, Aai doesn't want me? You'll say she's grown up now and even if she thinks like this she'll realise it's foolish. I understand, but I've become extraordinarily sensitive where Mimi is concerned. Things that other mothers say and do so easily, I think about fifty times over and finally keep them to myself. Don't you often say to Sujata, 'Come on, bestir yourself, see if you can get a scholarship'? And she laughs and sends off an application. If I were to try saying this to Mimi the words would stick in my throat, and if I did say them finally they would come out sounding so garbled it would be as good as not saying them at all. Didn't Janaki tell Madhu, 'Off you go now, stop clinging to your mother'? She literally bundled him off to Calcutta. But neither Sujata nor Madhu would ever think that you were throwing them out.

I don't know where I went wrong. When I want to draw them close and hug them, I think my daughters will say, 'Our mother wants to tie us to her apron strings.' And if I let them go their way I'm afraid they'll think, she's throwing us out! I know what you'll say now. She analyses things too much, that's what you'll say. Which is why I want you to do one thing. Meet Mimi, talk to her, find out what she really wants and then write and give me your opinion. I've already written to her to not take any decision until I return. I'll be back in four or five months anyway, so there's no great rush. But since she shares her thoughts so freely with you and Sujata, I'm giving you this responsibility. I'll be waiting for your letter. Otherwise all is well. (I mean, you'll say what's bloody well? That's also true) I'll speak about that when we meet.

— Shami, finish your bath quickly. It's getting late.
— Finished, finished! I just have to rinse off the soap. Keep my clothes ready.
— They're on the bed.
— Not these, I want my new frock.
— We're going by bus and train and it's the rush hour. Why do you want to wear your new clothes in all that pushing and shoving? Trousers and a shirt are better.
— I don't want them. Can I wear a salwar-kameez at least? I want to show it to Sujata.
— Okay, here they are. Come on, hurry up. And don't take a dupatta. It'll get entangled somewhere and tear, or strangle you.
— What fun is there in a salwar-kameez then?
— Oh, go on, wear whatever you want.
— No, you tell me.
— Listen, I put out what I thought you should wear. You say you don't want to, so wear what you like.
— No, you tell me.
— I will if you wear what I say.
— Okay.
— Jeans and a shirt.
— But it's so hot today!
— Then go naked. Or stay at home.

Dear Janaki,

Mimi left early this morning to go to her father in Canada. I can't tell you what a commotion the two of us made all night with our crying. You'll say – why did you send her away then? My dear, I've done so much thinking about it, I'm completely confused. But finally I thought, whatever I did for Mimi after deliberation turned out to be wrong somehow, so why not let her do what she wants? It's as if my hands are trapped under a rock – it hurts if I move them, and hurts if I don't. Let's see if she can move the rock herself. Her decision didn't change even while she was sobbing away. I kept saying, 'Mimi, you don't have to put up with any hardship. If you find it difficult or if you don't like it, just come back.' Shami joined us in sobbing now and then. God knows how Yaju stood it. When Mimi was leaving she first shook hands a little formally with Yaju, but then she couldn't help herself and she hugged him saying, 'Dada'. She cried too. On the whole I'm glad I decided to say goodbye to her at home so as to avoid a scene at the airport. I'm recovering now. At every step I feel her absence but I'll get used to it gradually. I'll visit you when I'm in some kind of state to talk and tell you things. Actually, I'll be uneasy till I hear from her that she's reached and is settling down. I can't help it. You must be worried about Madhu's exams so I won't write any more. My best wishes to him.

— You can't cut the nails of your right hand with your left hand!
— I know.
— Come here if you want me to cut them.
— Forget it.
— What?
— I said, forget it.
— What does that mean? Are you not going to cut the nails of your right hand until you're older and can do it yourself?
— I didn't mean that. I'll cut them tomorrow when you're not watching.
— And if you can't manage?
— Mimi or Dada will do it, whenever they come.
— Shami, don't be silly. There's two months more for Dada to come, and who knows about Mimi!
— It's okay. I'll just keep them clean.

— Yaju, can I say something? You've come after so long, I really don't want to bring up an unpleasant subject.

— It's about Shami!

— Yes.

— What is it?

— But please don't talk of 'other mothers' and make me feel bad – I don't have those qualities, so just let it go.

— Okay.

— You never reproach me with not being beautiful, think of this in the same way.

— I said, okay. You can cut out the preamble.

— Why don't we send Shami to a hostel?

…

— I can't cope any more. Every morning, the minute I get up, my tongue turns bitter. The same things every day, the same spats, the same questions and answers, the same grumbling and banging about. Then I get tired and stop speaking. For days together we don't speak to each other. But I'm seething inside and suddenly I erupt. Because she throws her clothes all over her room. Because she hasn't washed her hair. Because I tripped over the chappals she discarded at the door. Because, in spite of my telling her not to eat or drink in the living room, there are ants around her spilt cocoa. Because she comes home late after playing … But the truth is that there's no real 'because'. I get angry with her – that's all.

— But why do you get angry with her? I agree she pushes you to the limit and you have a bad temper. But over such trifles? And she's a child, isn't she…

— I accept that, I accept everything. But now, for her own good – or you can say it's to protect us from each other – we need to be apart.

— But …

— I've tried very hard, I no longer use angry, abusive words. But once something sets me off, it's like a fire has been lit. I know I shouldn't, but I can't stop speaking. She keeps looking at me sullenly, as if she's bored, and that makes me even more wild. Sometimes I'm afraid … And you're not here, you're always in another town or abroad.

— Then I'll take up another job, I'll stay here.

— What difference will that make? It'll be like our time in Japan again. I'll get even more angry because I'll feel she's creating rifts between us, that she's coming in the way of our happiness.

— I don't understand why it should be like this. Why don't you talk to someone? To Abhi Raj?

— But is it so abnormal to send her to a hostel? Why do we need to take Abhi Raj's advice?

— Not about the hostel, but about your anger. Especially because you're unable to cope with it and behave normally.

— Yaju, do you think I don't know this myself? I know the basics of psychology. What can Abhi Raj tell me that I don't know? He'll say a child is not a doll I can shape the way I want, and this is what I resent. That she's a being I've created but I can't control her, and so my ego is hurt. That I'm jealous because I'm moving into middle age and she's approaching youth. That, because of Mimi's problems, I neglected her when she was little, so she's jealous And, who knows, our getting to know each other and marrying so late in life and the fact that we've been able to live together for such short periods – maybe they are the cause of this mess as well.

— What are you saying?

— Yes, that's how it is. By this time, other couples our age would have already done most of the things they do as a couple, or the things they do without children. We started late. And I keep thinking – if we put aside these ten or fifteen years because of her, what's left for Yaju and me? If it was just Mimi, by this time she would have been off our hands and we would have had some good years left. But it'll be another ten or fifteen years before Shami is on her own, by which time we'll be past sixty. Then what's left? And if things go on like this we'll be wrecks, all of us.

— If you know all this ...

— I do, but I can't put it into practice.

— Listen, I've never made any difference between yours and mine, but when Mimi brought such a terrible situation upon us I survived, didn't I? I knew it was a question of your daughter's whole life, so I steeled myself and endured it stoically. Can't you do the same for my – for our – daughter?

— Yaju! You're a saint. I'm only a petty, selfish, cruel, useless woman.

— Why do you abuse yourself?

— This isn't abuse, I'm saying what I really think. Please protect her from me now. If it were possible, I would have said you and she, both of you, leave me and go. But it's impossible.

— Is it possible for me? Is it possible for me to leave you? I roam all over the world because I know you are living in some part of it. I go away to come back to you, to come home. Aren't you my home? Only you? Don't cry, I'm speaking the truth. Listen, I went away from Mimi and you after that incident – work was only an excuse. In fact I was alone in Manali. I used to wander about all day, thinking till I was exhausted. But I couldn't do it. I came back home. Not for Mimi or Shami, but for you. Don't cry, otherwise I'll start crying myself.

— Look, I'm not saying this to comfort you, but I think part of her stubbornness and troublesome nature comes from being alone. If she had had company we wouldn't have had this trouble. When she sees others doing things without any fuss in the hostel, she'll learn to do them herself. Besides, when she comes home for the holidays, she'll find her parents' rare presence welcome.

— In that case, you're not to fight with her in the holidays, not a word. Otherwise I'll take her off somewhere during her break.

— Promise, I promise. I won't say even one nasty word to her.

— Have you spoken to her?

— No, I thought I'd ask you first.

— How do we tell her?

— I've thought of that, too. We've already bought a piece of land in the village which Janubhayya urged us to buy. Let's build a house there. I don't want to live in the city – the chaos, the noise, the crowds make me feel insecure and useless. We were going to live there anyway – not right away, but some time later. What's wrong with building a house now?

— But how will I get leave for five or six months? You need at least that much time to build a house.

— You carry on with your travels. Tai, Bhayya and I will build it.

— And then?

— There's no school there – isn't that a good enough reason to send Shami away?

— Have you spoken to Bhayya yet? About where to apply? Then there's the problem of getting admission...

— We'll begin now. It'll happen in time – if all of us make up our minds to do it. And, Yaju ...

— What?

— Gradually we'll find each other again – won't we?

— We'll meet somehow. But whether it can be just you and me the way we were earlier, I don't know.

— What do you mean?

— How is it possible? Can we begin again as if nothing has happened? The two of us can meet only with the scars of defeat.

— That way, too. But it may also be a kind of growth. A person who is scared of defeat, who doesn't have any wounds, doesn't go to war. He'll have no scars at all. You have suffered wounds, so have I. I've accepted defeat, I've accepted that I have none of a woman's greatness, that whatever it is womanhood is made up of, it's not in me. But, finally, I'm trying to save her from being hurt. I don't mind if there's an emptiness in me which will never be filled. But not in her. At worst, she won't care about her mother; but at least she won't hate her and the world. A child's world is not very big or complex. You see how happy she is in school with her friends, books and movies – why, she's very happy with you, too! I'm the one who takes my own nagging to heart, not she. A hostel will be very good for her. Here, she'll only learn about meanness and wickedness as she grows up. This knot can't be unravelled, Yaju, it'll only become more complicated. Let's not make it worse.

— Then let's go and meet Tai and Bhayya tomorrow or the day after. We'll talk to them about everything.

When the idea of building a house came to us we decided that, since we were building it after having lived away for nearly half our lives, we would make it exactly the way we wanted. We wouldn't fill it up with just any odd thing – there would be no old or second-hand stuff, nothing bought casually or given to us because it was unwanted, etc. We would have beautiful things, carefully chosen, and just enough of them. And we would take our approaching old age into account and plan accordingly. We would have pleasing, rare colours inside the house, a flower and vegetable garden planted with love and enthusiasm, music so soft you scarcely heard it. And he and I. But ultimately, we had to make compromises everywhere, either because there wasn't enough money or enough time, or because we were not persistent enough, or couldn't take enough trouble. Besides, gifts given by friends who came to celebrate the new house added to the heterogenous medley of stuff in the house. For example: This lamp has been with us since my grandmother's time, it's a genuine antique. And the antique, an old broken lamp which didn't match anything in the house, ended up on the veranda. There were lots of such objects. Mimi was the last to come when the house was well set up. The moment she stepped in she began laughing. She said, 'Aai, this house is absolutely you! Exactly like all your other houses. If I'd been brought here blindfolded, I'd have recognised my Aaisaheb's house the moment I opened my eyes.'

I didn't know whether to laugh or cry. I remembered the times I had hurriedly set up house in different towns, in different countries. Each time I had resolved firmly that I didn't care if the house remained empty, I would not have makeshift, temporary, anything-will-do arrangements. But that's exactly what always happened. Chairs made from crates in which we'd packed books, tables from boxes, a bolster made out of a rolled-up mattress covered with a tablecloth, bedspreads and curtains made from old saris, shelves put up on bricks or upturned garden pots… And people who saw would exclaim: 'How do you get these ideas?' So is it surprising that this daughter of mine who grew up in diapers which matched the made-from-old-saris bedspreads should think that this was how her mother's house had to be? Middle-class poverty is awful. Real honest poverty is not ashamed of itself. We're the ones who love to make pista barfi from ridge gourd peel and almond sweets out of groundnuts, we roll up mattresses and cover them and grow plants in old Dalda tins. Is anyone fooled by this? Rich people's skins have a different sheen altogether. If you see a rich woman wearing a sari frayed at the edges you will say, 'Oh, she must have just torn it while getting out of the car.' Whereas all our efforts to darn or hide a tear are of no use; it's sure to be noticed. Besides, even if we fool the world we know the truth ourselves – that this is no bolster, but a mattress rolled up and covered with a tablecloth. Once, as a child, I had gone into a rich person's bathroom and seen the towels piled up there, thick towels in matching colours, all of them with the same design, but different shapes; I had resolved then that I would do exactly the same. But our bathroom contains all kinds of towels, from Turkish ones worn out through constant washing to the thin khadi kind. Two towels bought cheaply at a sale, four thin and narrow ones bought because they're good for drying hair, two big towels made into four for the children – after all, why did they need such big ones? – the cut edges left unstitched out of laziness. And so many more 'demoted' to being kept near the basin and then occasionally 'promoted' out of necessity. Ultimately I decided that matching towel sets were beyond me. Of course it was the same with plates, cups and saucers, pots and pans and sheets and pillow covers!

I drew my joyful laughing daughter close to me and said, 'I thought if it's too neat and shining you'll find it strange, you won't recognise it. That's why I kept everything the way it used to be.' And the girl then went round the house with her father looking fondly at familiar articles unearthed from various boxes, stuff which had not been discarded when we moved house.

She and this father of hers are collectors. What I have is my father's habit of getting rid of things. I had been furious with him when he'd exchanged the huge solid shining copper bathing vessel which had been in the family for generations, for plastic buckets. And yet I've been speaking fondly of this incident for the last few years. They say women like to collect trash, but I find great satisfaction in throwing stuff out of the house. Though I grumbled each time we moved there was also some satisfaction in thinking: now I can throw out the junk, everything will be neat and new, the way I want it … But the truth is that each house, yes, even this one, has been the same all over again. Mimi was right.

Dear Shami,

So, how are things, Chhamchham? I believe you're grown-up now. I hear you're leaving Aai-Dada and going to the hostel. That there's no good school near their new home and all that is only an excuse. I know everything! You're bored at home, aren't you? I used to get bored, too, feel lonely. Now you'll have loads of friends in the hostel. And enemies too – to get intimate with and fight with with gusto. Have fun, okay? I only had two years in the hostel, but I can't tell you what fun it was! Company in everything, from secret midnight snacks to studying. Once, we tied a spider to a string just above Sister's head. What an uproar there was when she woke up. First her shouts, then ours. Shall I tell you something else? If you study hard, I'll pester Aai-Dada to send you here after you've finished school. Okay? So have fun and write about it to me. Don't forget.

Your
Mimi

A huge scare today! Shami brought a puppy home from the village and when she was feeding it, it bit her. I was so scared that I said all sorts of things to her. Like: 'Now you'll get rabies,' 'I've told you a thousand times that stray dogs are dangerous, but you never listen,' 'Now you'll have to get fourteen injections in your tummy,' 'If you get rabies, it means sure death', and so on. I didn't notice that Shami was steadily getting more and more nervous. Finally she cried out, 'Dada' and began to bawl and then I started crying as well. Seeing this chaotic scene, Sonubai had the presence of mind to send for Yaju, but with all the sobbing going on he couldn't make out what had happened and to whom. Once he got it, he just bundled the dog, Shami and me into the jeep and took us to Biju. Obviously, she berated me first. But I've been terrified of wild dogs since childhood and I wasn't prepared to listen to anything. After I'd finished demanding that we go to Mumbai right away, she said, 'Mavshi, will you now allow the doctor to handle this? Leave the dog here and take Shami home. I don't think it has rabies but if it does, it'll show up in three or four days and then you can go to Mumbai. Okay?'

While we were talking a man came in and asked, 'Why has the doctorbai taken our dog and tied it up?' When we heard that it was his pet dog and that it had had all the necessary injections, my face was worth seeing. I didn't want Yaju and Biju to make fun of me, not in front of Shami, so I went out quickly and sat quietly in the jeep. Yaju, when he came with Shami five or ten minutes later, was laughing loudly. 'What is it now?' I asked. And he told me that Shami thought that if you were bitten by a dog, you got 'babies' and that after they had 'babies', people died and they were given injections in their stomachs so that they wouldn't die. After all, babies were in the stomach!

When Shami saw me laughing as well, she was furious. I said, 'You'll be going to school soon, so don't you make such an exhibition of your stupidity there!' So much for my having given her clear and scientific answers to all her doubts about babies! And now, when she goes to school, the nuns will tell her, 'God puts babies into you,' which will confuse her even further. I said, 'When you have kids you can be sure I'll tell them this 'rabies' story!'

Shami's holidays got over today and she's gone back to school. Since I didn't want any quarrels in the house, I kept strict control over my tongue the entire vacation. Perhaps because I'd given Yaju my word, or maybe I'd just lost the habit of bickering, or no longer had the urge to fight. Anyway, the holidays passed off peacefully on the whole. She had quite a number of activities too – looking after new plants, learning to ride on Superman, the pony which was bought with such enthusiasm, going on her bike to meet Ashu-Samir, teaching the puppies something or the other. In a way, the holidays passed swiftly but when she was leaving, I (and she too?) sighed with relief.

Why is it like this? Is it the same with everyone? I get on well with my daughters when they're away but I don't want to be with them every day. And yet, don't Tai and Viru-Biju get on all the time? And Ranju and Sujata or Janaki and Madhu? I must be lacking in motherliness. Mimi sometimes, though rarely, used to speak angrily of 'other mothers'. Shami is still a little girl. Poor thing, she prays every night the way the nuns have taught her to: 'God bless my father and my mother and my sister and Superman.' I'm the one who sometimes gets fed up and tells her, 'Why don't you get yourself a mother who will love you with her whole heart?' And she says, 'But I have you!' When she cries herself to sleep after one of our fights, I feel very sorry for her. Poor things, so unlucky to have a mother like me. Thank God, they have a loving father. Ever since I gave him my word last year I don't fight with her, as far as possible, I don't lash out at her with my tongue. What had Abhi said some years back? 'You use words so brilliantly to make her feel how useless she is. Is that what your intelligence is for?' I was bitterly ashamed of myself. But then it would begin all over again. I would grit my teeth and call her useless. I came to my senses only when her father threatened to take her and leave. Doesn't that make me useless? When I read of an American woman who held her child's hand in the fire, I'd exclaimed, 'What cruelty!' But wasn't my behaviour just as cruel?

But all this is on paper. If she provokes me, those fiery words will come to my tongue again. Anyway, it's enough that I've learnt to contain them within me. Why do I get so angry with her – with both of them? How will we ever know, before we really become mothers, whether we are fit for motherhood? I'd once said to Janubhayya that it would have been good if there were a kind of exam for it, like an M.A. or something, and he said, 'You had Mimi. Wasn't that enough of an examination?' But simple fool that I was, I thought – when Mimi was born I had many problems, so many things went wrong that I never experienced that feeling of motherliness; we were equals in all things. But this time I'll do everything right, textbook fashion. And it was like that till Shami was about four or five. God knows what went wrong after that. Nothing worked. Quarrels all the time, shouting and yelling, threats, sulks, anguish. Is it because I realised how useless I was as a mother that I itched to call her 'useless, stupid, wicked'?

How is it with other people? On the face of it, it seems to work fine for everyone else. Mothers and children love one another, fathers seem to be fond of them – how, then, do you ask them this question? I've spoken of my anguish to Ranju, Janaki, Tai. Ranju and Janaki are dear friends, they're my age and so, to some extent, they're on my side. They said natures differ, that I take childhood misdeeds too hard, that I analyse actions and words too much. But what it boiled down to was this: I am not real mother-material. Tai didn't soften the blow. She told me, very frankly, that even taking into account the fact that children's natures differ, the root of my failure was that I was too self-centred.

And yet, aren't there a lot of self-centred people in the world? Somebody should conduct classes in motherhood for them. Before I became a mother I had thought that this new experience, this new person, would fill some gap in my life, that I would become more complete, that one of my life's potentials would now be realised, and so on. But what happened was just the opposite. Because of the children all my activities were curtailed. I began to wonder whether we shouldn't deduct fifteen or twenty years from our lives on account of them. No going out, no seeing anything, not even just simple reading and writing. Keep yourself ready for fulfilling the children's demands – that is all! Since it was my lot, since it was inevitable, I did everything, grumbling all the while, and once the novelty wore off, with anger. Is this that same anger?

To whom can I speak of this? Ultimately, only to myself. In this world everyone will say – you took it on knowingly, now go through with it. But when I see what the children and I suffer as we go through with it, I think one must speak the truth some time. Don't go on praising motherhood – say that it is boring, repetitive, constricting and devastating, both for the mind and the body. Does everyone know this truth, and is this why they cloak it with fond admiration, praise, love and regard? Did my grandmother get angry with my mother? My mother with me? I think now that she did. Perhaps she didn't have as much anger as I do, or maybe she had more control over herself, but it was there. Yes. Tai says she was very scared of our mother. And when I was little, even if I wasn't afraid, I did think it was better to avoid her. Is motherhood like the story about Maruti's umbilicus then, something that everybody knows the truth about, but no one will say it out aloud?

— What are you doing today, Yaju?
— It's watering time for the acacias, I have to start with that.
— Will you check whether the beans are ready to be propped up? Let me know if they are, I'll send Sakhubai with the string.
— Hmm.
— And then?
— Then?
— After the watering?
— Get the acacia grove weeded.
— And after that?
— I need to look at the groundnuts in Biju's field, then pack the cucumber seeds Tai wants in bags. After which I'll come back for lunch.
— I didn't ask for a timetable, Yaju.
— Sorry.
— You haven't asked me what I'm doing today.
— What are you doing today?
— It's bread day today, isn't it? I have to bake bread for everyone.
— Good! Which means you'll be in a good mood by the afternoon.
— Why?
— When you're kneading dough you seem to get the same satisfaction as if you were pounding your enemies! Which means you'll be in a good mood in the afternoon.
— What do you mean! I'm always in a good mood, you're the irritable one.
— Then I'll have to find work which provides an outlet for my emotions – like your bread-making.

— Look for it then!
— What?
— I won't tell you! You'll reject whatever I suggest, you're so contrary. No guessing where your daughter gets that trait from!
— Then I'll decide myself or I'll ask Bhayya. At least he doesn't think that I'm bad-tempered like you do.
— I didn't mean that, Yaju. Now don't …
— What else? In just four sentences you made me out to be rude, irritable and cussed.
— No! If I say *you're* bad-natured, where will I find any good-natured people? Please don't be angry, Yaju, I was only joking.
— Sorry, I seem to have become really irritable, I can't even take a joke now. There, add another bad quality to your list.
— Yaju, please, you don't have any bad qualities. I have this habit of chattering unnecessarily, that's why I pester you. It's just the two of us now. I'll learn to read your thoughts from looking at your face. But until I learn, I'll have to ask you. What kind of bread shall I bake for you?
— French.
— Okay. We'll have a treat today! Fresh new French bread and cheese and soup made with home-grown vegetables.
— Absolute luxury! If Bhayya comes, ask him to stay. Otherwise, ring up Tai and invite them both.
— Can't it be just the two of us?
— Of course. But if Tai and Bhayya come you'll be free to chatter!
— Fine. And they can take their bread with them – saves us a trip.
— Done then! See you at lunch.

I'm beginning to abandon my belief that language is used to make conversation possible, or to express our feelings to others, or that it helps a person behave in a certain way. We say one thing and the listener hears something else. Even a simple, straightforward sentence like, 'Do what you want' has so many meanings that it's no use saying it at all. Because you then have to explain it as follows: 'What I really want to say is this'; 'Don't look for other meanings in it…'; etc. And then you think, what if I say nothing at all? What if I decide to use language only for things like, 'Come and eat,' or, 'The water is hot,' or 'Shall we send the gourds to the market?' Will I then acquire the art of understanding what's in the mind without using words? Why do I chatter so much when there is really nothing to say? Is it to make sure, by hearing my own voice, that I'm alive? And since this is not mere 'sound', like mewing or chirping, the listener tries to find meaning in the sound – i.e., in the words. After which, it's total confusion. Does Yaju not speak because he has nothing to say? Or has he, because of such thoughts, reduced his need for speech? Did Yaju 'speak' formerly? Before Mimi? Before Shami? I can't remember now, but even his 'not-speaking' becomes significant because I'm looking at it in the context of language. This needs to be changed. A person who doesn't speak, doesn't speak; one should leave it at that. We analyse what is spoken as well as what is not – this is the compulsion language has imposed on us. I must liberate myself from this. If I feel a very powerful urge, I should write letters to myself!

Today this house celebrated one more birthday. We opened one of the wine bottles we'd saved for just such a happy occasion – a birthday, or perhaps an anniversary. In the evening we watched the sunset through the now quite well-grown eucalyptus trees. Looking at the sun making its way between the large barren clouds gathered on the horizon, we raised our

glasses to each other and sipped our wine. And then he asked,
— So how do you feel?
— I'm still a little scared, can't say that I've got used to this decision.
— Do you think you'll be able to go through five more years?
— Yes. And you?
— Easily. That's what I think – at this moment, anyway.
— Okay, then. Here's to the next five.

We sat outside talking of various things until the moon came up and it became chilly. On my way to bed I stopped at my desk and opened my diary; he stopped, too, and touching the five or six diaries on the top shelf said,
— Well, there are quite a few diaries now, aren't there? What have you written?
— Open them and read.
— No, thanks! I'd rather read my history of China.
— That's likely to be more interesting. What will you find in my diaries? Today we plucked the melons from the big field, today Soni had her kittens – that's all!
— What! Is that all? No haikus for lovers, no profound thoughts about life's experiences? No pithy passages about places and journeys? No description of the cycle of the seasons?
— If you look carefully you may find a recipe or two, or the depth of Janubhayya's deep well. But if you want lovers, I'll have to hunt out some guys. That is, if you want my diaries to compete with China's history.
— You'll have to go quite far to find them, won't you?

He gave the diaries one more smiling glance and, with a little tap on my head, went away. But my gaze lingered on the diaries. They were beautiful, all alike, the paper inside fine; Dick had sent them to me, one each Christmas for the last six years. Each month had a picture of a sixteenth or seventeenth century sailing ship. When I told him I loved the first one he sent and had made a new year resolution to scribble something in it at least once or twice a week, if not every day, the diaries began arriving every Christmas.

As I was writing this, I thought: if Dick had really been my lover would the world have seen this decent man Yaju living with me so happily – well, almost so happily? He would have turned his back on me long ago.

Things keep happening and at some point you think, Hey! all this has happened before. When my mother used to call me by my sister's name, I would get furious: What is this, am I a nobody? But now I do the same thing, I call our older daughter by the younger one's name. Not only that, I call various friends, nephews, grandchildren and sons-in-law by my husband's name. It's a curious thing about names – all of us think our names are our very own. Yes, even people with names as ordinary as Anil and Ashok. Now look at my name – it isn't very unusual. At one time it had been in fashion and so it's quite common in a certain age group. Nevertheless I get really annoyed if it's spelt wrongly on a magazine cover. Does this make any sense? Firstly, it's a Marathi name; people can spell it whichever way they like. Why should I insist that it be written exactly the way I do? But one's name becomes as much a part of one's personality as the nose on one's face. Actually, I have many complaints against my name: it's harsh, it doesn't sound soft or sweet, it can't be converted into a fond pet name, and so on. Yaju (as usual) has found a simple way out of this; he never calls me by my name. If I'm with him, he says 'you', if I'm not, he says 'you' a bit more loudly. That's it! On the other hand, I love using names. I use the name of the person I'm speaking to in every second sentence; I became aware of this mannerism of mine because the girls made fun of it the other day. No chance of my improving now!

To be honest I have no faith in improvement. Nobody improves, neither humans, nor nations, nor cultures. Is it an improvement because we have found cures for a few diseases? Is it progress if we trade in some problems or some kinds of suffering for others?

On the other hand, look at Ranju: she has immense faith in progress. She believes that all of us will improve, that relationships between people will definitely get better – if not in this life, then in the next. And so she goes on forming new relationships. I'm always amazed by optimists; does one applaud them or ridicule them? They resolutely ignore what they see and go on being incurably optimistic. This is worth praising. Because what do pessimists like me do except give up and think such thoughts? This year we've not had even our usual pathetic four or five inches of rain, we have just enough water for the house. All our vegetable beds have been abandoned. And so, telling myself with my usual hopelessness, 'I have done my duty,' I sit on the veranda idly looking at the barrenness outside with despair. But Fate has given me a husband who is a great optimist. (No, actually I got him on my own, happily, willingly and cleverly.) And so, when I looked at his various activities, all of them meant to save water as well as the garden, I felt ashamed of myself and got up to give him a helping hand.

Dear Yoshiyo and Hisayo,

I've just got your letter today, telling me that you'll be holidaying in Hawaii this year. I'm disappointed. I had hoped that you would spend at least a week if not your entire vacation with us, either on your way to or from Europe. But if it's Hawaii that means you won't come this way at all. You must *come next year, I won't take 'no' for an answer. If you don't agree, I'll send you my anger instead of the best wishes I always send with Yaju. Anyway, enjoy your holidays and send a nice card to this stay-at-home.*

I never thought I'd be so disappointed that Yoshiyo and Hisayo could not come. When it happened I thought, of course I'm fond of them; but am I also disappointed because I'm bored with the monotony here? If Yaju asks me to now, I'll go with him, never mind where, for a change. I may not have made friends with many women in different parts of the world, but I certainly got to know them well enough to spend a few hours chatting and laughing with them. But not in Japan. Just when I had begun to wonder whether Japanese women have any existence apart from their husbands and children, I met Hisayo. Which is why I'm so fond of her. They are the only couple who became our friends. They had no children so had fewer entanglements to keep them at home, which made it much easier for them to join us on our various trips. They often pressed invitations on Shami to go to their place – that was when Shami's and my relationship was deteriorating by the day. If it didn't reach rock bottom it's because of the time Shami spent with them. By nature, the Japanese abhor plumbing the depths of emotion. So, without probing too much, they accepted us as we were, the way we seemed to be; this too is part of their attraction for me. Maybe that's why the many-faceted qualities of my friendship with Toshi, for instance, didn't become part of our relationship with both of them. Anyway, I have memories of many moments of happy togetherness with them. In short, I think they're the only two among all my friends and relations of whom the only memories I have are of happy friendship. I have told myself I will get them here next year even if I have to harness them. Yaju laughs at my great desire and says, you built a house in this place to get away from the world and now you want the whole world to come here. What do you call this?

Dear Dada,

Thanks for your birthday wishes. Your complaint that I haven't brought home a son-in-law to augment the male population of our family is valid. But let me be honest: I'm searching for an adorable husband like you, so it's not easy. Jokes apart, let me tell you the truth: I have found someone like that, someone unique. (I know you'll exclaim at this!) He teaches art and photography at a school here. He is Indian and his name is Vinay. I know that at this point Aai will say – 'This girl has to be different. Two generations of us married people outside our caste, region, religion, even country – and this girl goes back to the old story!' But he's a lovely man. (Handsome, too, in my opinion. I'll send pictures in a day or two.) And most important, he happily solved two very knotty problems of mine. One: no children. (In this matter I've accepted yours and Aai's lesson to do good to the world!) And the second: that I would travel all over the world on account of my work in search of news, and he would look after the home. He agreed immediately. Isn't that grand? But the real *reason is that I've fallen in love with him. I know that my joy will make you happy. I'm urging him to spend some of the treasure he's accumulated in the bank and come home with me, but he has this one innate shortcoming. I'll drag him along the next time I come home.*

With lots of love. (When you fall in love, you accumulate loads of it inside you, so I have lots to send you both!)

Mimi

I'm still recovering from the shock I got on seeing the photo of Vinay's that Mimi sent us. He's a victim of thalidomide; he has only one arm with a hand attached to the shoulder. He uses his feet to do whatever we do with our hands. When I opened the letter and saw his photograph, the house began whirling about me and I fell off my chair. Yaju tells me that Anna, who was working in the garden, rushed in on hearing Sonubai's screams and helped her put me on the bed. And then there began a frantic scurrying about. By the time Yaju came from the grove I was sitting up; I had no strength to do anything else. When Yaju saw the photo he totally ignored me and said, 'Aha! Our son-in-law is very handsome; we can say he's the best of all sons-in-law.' And after making some excuse to Sonubai and Anna he went back to work, leaving me with the photograph.

Slowly, I forced myself to look at it. My eyes kept moving to the dreadful deformity near his shoulder, but I dragged them elsewhere. And I saw that he had a very good looking and smiling face. But there was much more besides. Grief and determination and compassion. Mimi had taken this picture, so he must have been looking straight at her. And I wondered – was the compassion for her? I marvelled at him. Slowly I began remembering little things about my Mimi. When she was small she was mine alone, it was she for me and I for her. We endured shocks and blows, we counted every paisa, we raged at each other, we grumbled – but we were together and we ran home to be with each other. Sometimes we had fun, at other times we were troubled. She was about seven or eight when I met Yaju. Once, when Yaju took my side during a quarrel between us and tried to make peace, she retorted sharply, 'You met her only yesterday but I've known her since I was born – you need not defend her!' And she stomped out in a rage when we laughed.

How did the girls, whom I brought up with such love, suddenly move away from my life? Shami began this process when she was only four; but Mimi seemed to be mine until she was quite grown-up, and because she was mine she was like me as well. I get angry if I'm asked too many questions so I don't ask questions of others, either. Who knows what Mimi made of this! Did she think her mother wasn't interested in her? I never questioned her directly or even indirectly about anything because I thought she might look upon it as interference. I never ever rang up her friends if she came home late (remembering how humiliated I used to feel when my mother did this). I did worry a lot, and felt bad that she never confided in me herself. But I presented a calm front, trained myself to listen to what she told me without making too much of it. Did this make her think her mother didn't care? It's no use worrying about all this now, but what if I had probed more deeply, grumbled and nagged her? Would I still have had the various shocks I've had since? Like when she spent the money for her fees on a film. (Yaju said, 'All children do such things at some time or other. It's not as if she's robbed or murdered someone!') Or when I saw her smoking at the age of fifteen. (Yaju said, 'What a puritan you are. Children always do these things on the sly.') Or when she was eighteen and said, Yaju is trying to seduce me and told her friends colourful stories about it. (This time even Yaju was shaken.) Somehow she finished college and, escaping to Canada, became a news photographer. (Yaju said nothing, but when she returned he took her advice about what kind of camera to buy to replace his old one.) And now this! I sometimes think Mimi must be someone else's daughter. Such things happen to 'others', not to us! We should have had children like the others, brought them up, cared for them, educated them, and set them on the road to marriage and careers without any fuss – this should have been 'our lot'. I have only two daughters. One of them has done what 'others' should be doing; and as for the other, don't even ask! If I say the sun rises in the East she will say no, in the West, and if I say, yes, of course, it rises in the West she'll say, how come you don't even know these simple things? You're stupid!

And now Vinay. Why did Yaju ignore my distress, my anguish? If I ask him he'll say, because you should understand it yourself. To some extent I do understand. Mimi's is a loving nature – she's eager not only to be loved, but to love as well; she respects Vinay's enormous courage, she knows how much she needs that kind of dogged strength herself … What else? When I meet them I will know the 'what else'.

When I see pictures of the two of them taken by a friend I want to weep, though it cheers me up as well. Vinay on the beach playing ball with his feet, Mimi laughing heartily as she looks at him. Mimi throwing a grape from a distance into his open mouth, Mimi leaning against his shoulder and looking at him with narrowed eyes. (In this picture, the hand which comes out of his shoulder is on her shoulder and she is leaning her cheek on it.) What shall I write to Mimi? I should send her my book and write: Your mother loves you very much but she is unable to say this to you, therefore this attempt at poetry. I don't have the confidence to translate my thoughts into simple words and so this ubiquitous device. Will she understand?

My darling mother,

Who gave you permission to fall ill? What are you up to? Why don't you take care of yourself? And just what is 'your Yaju' doing in Hong Kong at this time? Call him back immediately, otherwise I'll come there myself and kidnap you. Understand? You're our one and only mother and one and only mothers are not allowed to fall ill. Okay? At least go to Mavshi's until you're better. If I don't hear from you in a fortnight (I'm giving the postal departments of both countries a chance to show their swiftness!) I'll begin a telegraphic assault. Remember this and get well soon.

Your
Mimi

Aaa…iii, you've really written a book of poetry! Amazing! Why was this concealed for so long? Do we have to hear from Biju that it got a prize? Right now, it's poetry, soon it will be stories and novels. No need to look back, you're going to be famous. Sorry, I should say more famous, shouldn't I? Vinay doesn't know enough Marathi, he can't even manage to read, so it's my duty to translate but I don't have enough skill to cope. I know he'll pester you when he meets you.

This year's Christmas card is his doing. It's a picture of a small pond and a hill behind our house. He specialises in water colours – delicate, gentle pastels. The exhibition will most probably be next March or April – we'll be with you before that. I tell him that he can't paint his kind of pictures in the area around our house; for that he needs clear primary colours, strong definite lines. He's very eager to see it all. I wanted to escape the winter here, but there's a lot of work. Most probably we'll come in April. I'll let you know as soon as it's definite. Congratulations again.

P.S. Re-reading my letter I realise I hadn't congratulated you in the first place. But, as the Mad Hatter says, you can do a thing 'again' without having done it at all!

I had been very troubled by how to talk and behave with Mimi and Vinay when they came, but my doubts vanished the moment I saw him. He gave me a big smile, quickly came to me and 'hugged' me. After which I quite forgot that he had any deformity, or that he was different. Once we had settled down after coffee etc., he said, 'Please ask me anything you want to about me without hesitation.' He was drinking his coffee by bending very low and, without lifting the cup, tilting it towards himself with the 'hand' attached to his shoulder. I didn't know what to say. But Yaju bluntly asked, 'Why don't you remove this hand and get an artificial arm instead? It should be possible, at least on the left.'

'I've been thinking of that for the last few years, but for one thing, it costs too much. And, secondly, I'm very reluctant to give up what I've got used to and begin getting used to something new. We're going to get compensation from the government; it may be possible then. But to be honest, I'm a little scared – I wonder whether my art, which comes from my 'hand', can be transferred to an artificial limb.'

Then Mimi said, 'Vinay, your art is in you, not in your "hand".'

'Let's see whether I can keep this hand as it is and get an artificial arm on the left.' He said no more.

Shami then asked, 'Do you really draw pictures with your foot? Will you show me?'

I was going to exclaim, 'Shami!' when he replied quickly, 'Shami, this is not a circus. And there's nothing extraordinary about it. My foot is my hand. It's in a different place, that's all! You draw pictures with your hand – do you even think about it? I'm going to draw some pictures in a few days and you can see how I do it, okay? But before that I'm going to take pictures of all of you – lots of pictures. Do you like taking pictures, like Mimi?'

And then Mimi and he told us many interesting stories about a news photographer's life. How they have to take off for any part of the world where events worth photographing are happening, take pictures and sell them to different newspapers. Floods and famines, accidents and summit meetings, sports and war. On the whole, Vinay said, it was difficult and dangerous.

'I'm better off, I stay at home and draw pictures. Let Mimi do all the rushing about.'

Mimi said, 'I love the excitement. And when I come home, the sweetness of just sitting peacefully with Vinay is wonderful.'

After which the two of them looked at each other and laughed – such hearty and lovely laughter that Yaju and I, too, looked at each other and laughed in happiness.

When we went for a walk in the evening the girls went ahead with their father, walking on either side of him, dancing about him. When he tried to speak to one of them the other called out, 'Dada, Dada,' and drew his attention to herself. Typical! I was with Vinay. I said to him, 'We're such a small family but we're very rarely together. Most often the four of us are in four different corners. Tai, Bhayya and their children and grandchildren are with me more often.'

Perhaps my voice carried a hint of regret because he said softly, 'We shape our lives, they do the same – haven't you ever thought of it that way? The four of you have to live in four different corners, which is why you are like *this.* And because you are like this, it was easy for you to live in different corners, it seemed natural to you.'

'What do you mean by, like *this*?'

He began to laugh. 'Like this! You have feelings, but you don't reveal them. Or you write poetry.' I looked at him in surprise but he went on, not letting me speak: 'And if others try to impose their feelings on you, you escape. Within a fortnight Mimi gets bored with my love, my peacefulness, my regular routine of shopping and eating meals at the right time; in fact she gets bored with my domesticity and runs away – to Africa, to Russia or to Iran and Afghanistan or China and India.'

I smiled, too. And I thought, of course he's clever, but fortunately he's not tame. Only controlled. After we walked on a little further, I quickly asked him the question that had been going around in my mind. 'Vinay, what was your mother like? Didn't she give up everything for you? I couldn't even bring up two healthy, clever and pretty girls, how did she …?'

He said with some surprise, 'Didn't you? But they're lovely girls, aren't they? I like them.'

'They're good because of their own qualities. I have no share in that.'

'Aai! What do you mean? Mimi goes on all day about "Aai this" and "Aai that".'

'Well, leave that. Tell me about your mother.'

He was silent for a while, then said, 'In a way, she was like many other mothers but she used to feel guilty, she thought it was because of her mistake that her son was the way he was. She struggled to bring me up like other children as far as possible; but she ran around all the time to help me. That wasn't good for me. I began to think that all I had to do was sit in one place and the world would do everything for me.'

'Then?'

'My teachers asked both of us to go for special counselling. By that time a panel of special counsellors had been instituted for such cases. I went to a special school and hostel for thalidomide babies, as they advised. I was there till I completed high school. And so my mother could live without carrying a burden of guilt all the time, and I learnt to live without anger and bitterness. I met many people far more handicapped than I was, both physically and mentally, I learnt to do things for myself without help. And if an able person wanted to help me I learnt to take that help cheerfully, without getting angry with them or thinking myself inferior. I literally learnt to stand on my own two feet.' And he began laughing.

I was amazed that not only did Vinay not consider himself inferior, he was proud of himself. Impulsively I said to him, 'To me the biggest disadvantage of your not having arms and hands is that I can't hold your hands in joy.'

He too smiled as he said, 'That's absolutely true.'

That night I said to Yaju, 'Our son-in-law is the best son-in-law in the world.' And Yaju said with a laugh, 'That's absolutely true.'

When Vinay left after two weeks my eyes were wet with tears. In two days, Mimi would also leave after celebrating Shami's birthday and Shami would go back to school. The four of us would be living in four different corners of the world again.

Dear Dr Abhi Raj,

I'm writing after a long time, and once again about your 'favourite patient'. I had spoken to you about Mimi before I went to Japan and you told me very emphatically, 'Mimi is absolutely all right. Don't worry about her.' Since then I've given up that futile occupation. Later, when she was going to Canada, your rather impatient advice to my, 'What shall I do?' was, 'She's an adult now. Why do you want to analyse each action of hers? If, after thinking it over, she decides she wants to live in a certain way she should be allowed to, don't you agree? Do you run to the hospital each time you have a cold just because you had pneumonia or typhoid when you were a child? Stop worrying about her now.'

I've always kept this advice in mind. And so the good news. Mimi is married. The two of them are here. They will be leaving in another fortnight and I have asked her to meet you. You will like Mimi's husband a lot – that's all I will say right now. I like him even more than Mimi. You've met Shami just once or twice when you came home; she's doing well too. The most important thing is that within a short time of going to the hostel, the girl began quarrelling with various people. In my opinion, a person who has enough self-confidence to fight with others (and to end the quarrel as well) is very sane and will do well in this world. Why don't you come here for a few days for a respite from your strenuous life?

— Mimi, will you come with me to school tomorrow?
— No, I'm leaving early in the morning, I have to catch the Deccan Queen. Sorry.
— That's all right. But it's such fun when you're here, otherwise it's boring. Aai keeps nagging, Dada is busy with something or the other. And I can't visit Viru-Biju, they are so involved in their work and friends. The only thing I can do is roam around on Superman or on the bike. There's nothing else.
— Isn't it a good thing you went to the hostel? Didn't I say so? Lots of friends there, older girls to take care of you. And the nuns…
— Hey, we're the big girls now.
— Is that so, granny? So you're big now, are you? Then you should have learnt to behave sensibly! Why do you find Aai such a pain?
— She never stops. Do this, do that, why have you done this, don't do that…
— What's wrong with that? I've been watching you these last few days – you don't do a thing without being told and when you're told, you sulk. Do you behave the same way with the Sisters and Matron?
— No.
— So you behave well with others but not with Aai, huh?
— Now don't you start!
— Well, think about it yourself. Getting angry, refusing to talk, nobody likes that. What if Aai and Dada made a sour face the moment they saw you and said, 'Two months of boredom now!' Would you like that? Would it make you feel good?
— Yes, it would. Anyway they cheer up only when they see you, you're their favourite.
— Shami, don't be silly! You're the lucky one. You're not only *their* favourite, you're mine as well. But why don't you try to behave a little better? You say you're grown up, why do you create problems every day?

— I don't know, I don't understand. It's the way I am.
— Come on, try to be good. Promise, and I'll tell you a secret.
— I promise. What's the secret?
— Dada and Aai are going to send you to me during your holidays when you finish your twelfth.
— Wow! Fantastic! Really?
— But only if you behave. Got it? I'll be coming off and on and I'll take you only if I see an improvement. Okay? And tell me, what do you mean by saying you've grown up? Have you got your periods?
— Hah!
— What do you mean, hah? Do you know everything?
— Come on, I knew long back.
— Long back? Remember 'rabies'?
— Of course! But growing up on a farm has its uses, Didisaheb. Birds and bees, flowers and trees.
— Okay, then. If you have any doubts, ask Aai or ask me. Don't listen to the girls in school, okay? And if you're so clever, try to be clever in the right way. Now goodnight.
— Goodnight, Mimi. And wake me up before you go.

This year all of us – Yaju, Tai, Janubhayya, I and the house – had the digit five in our birthdays, so we celebrated them all together on Yaju's birthday which falls somewhere in between. There was quite a big gathering. After the weekend guests and all those who had come for the party – the children, their spouses, grandchildren, Dada, Vahini, and the few people who live close enough to be called neighbours – had gone, only Janubhayya, Tai and the two of us were left. This was three or four days back. It was monsoon time and the lake had enough water in it to make us feel optimistic. We chatted about various things, like how barren this place was when we came; Tai recalled how we never met anyone then but now whole colonies have sprung up. It's called a village, but politicians come from Mumbai for the panchayat elections. We spoke of many such things. Actually, it was just a way of dealing with the exhaustion which follows after being with too many people, a way of enjoying our easy intimacy. But we could as well have been silent.

Suddenly Janubhayya said, 'Well, Yaju, have you made your Will?'

'Shrujan, you're the limit, what a time …' Tai began, but Yaju simply said, 'Yes, everything goes to Biju and Viru.'

Janubhayya sat up straight. 'Why is that? Why to them? Mimi and Shami …'

I interrupted quickly to say, 'Mimi is over there and Shami may go as well. What use is this money to them? You can't take it there.'

And then the two of us got into an argument, Yaju and Tai putting in their two bits. My point was that parents shouldn't leave anything to their children. Janubhayya doesn't argue for the sake of arguing, or for an ideology. He went directly to the personal: 'Didn't you gladly accept whatever your parents left you?'

'They didn't want to leave us anything, either. They said a good education is the best legacy. They never thought that the house they built by saving every paisa would become so valuable. And though we did take what they left us, we also saved as much as possible for their own grandchildren and great-grandchildren and for some of their good works.'

'But if parents shouldn't leave anything to their children, why should an aunt do so?'

Then Yaju said, 'We're not giving anything to Biju and Viru personally. We want them to use it for their different social activities – to be used when needed. Okay?'

But Janubhayya wouldn't stop muttering, kept repeating

'something for Mimi-Shami ...' Finally I said, 'If you're going to make such a big thing of it, you draw up the Will and we'll sign it.'

The matter ended there, but I did think: even if our parents had left us nothing, we would still have thought they had given us a great deal. Whereas our children say – we didn't ask you to give birth to us! If someone gives you life should you be grateful to them, or rage at them? How many things can you hold your parents responsible for, apart from your birth and looks? When a man kills a complete stranger they say it's because his mother didn't love him, or his father was an alcoholic, or his mother punished him because he wet his bed at night as a child, or because she left him in an orphanage ... Nobody psychoanalyses Einstein and says that his great intellect was the result of his mother kissing him every day! 'The hand that rocks the cradle' and all that is fine, but *which* great man genuinely believes that he owes his greatness to his mother? If our faults and bad qualities are 'because of such parents', our greatness is always 'in spite of such parents'!

And what do parents think about their children? Is it 'because of' or 'in spite of'? I don't know what Yaju's 'other mothers' think, but my view is it's 'in spite of'. I had thought, after listening to paeans of praise on motherhood, that I too would be that kind of mother – soft, maternal, smiling but firm, stern when necessary, and so on. But the list remained just that, a list, and every day of being a mother made my tongue more venomous, my voice more harsh, each day brought new frowns on my face and new furrows on my forehead .... In spite of having children I completed my education, took up a job, greedily absorbed knowledge about various things, had experiences, read, saw, stubbornly refused to give up the relationship I had achieved with my dear husband, *in spite of* . . .

And I paid an exorbitant price for it. I loved – and the demands on love, on my time and energy went on increasing. When I tried to impose some discipline I received an impudent reply in an angry voice. Startled, I drew back and raised my hand – but reminding myself that this was not my way, I let it drop. My silence met with silence, my anger with anger, my hysteria with contempt, and my compromises with indifference. By the same logic, should not love have been met with love? But mothers are supposed to love their children, there's nothing unusual about that. And the love has to be undemanding. Which means that I lack the quality of motherhood in the same way that I am totally deficient in the art of drawing. As my Ajji used to say, 'When that particular quality was being distributed, I was in the toilet'! 'Other mothers' have that quality, as Yaju says. Tai for example. From the time her children were born till now, there has been no ill will between them. And how wonderful those children are! Is this Tai's success or were her children born this way? But if you're sensible you don't compare yourself to Tai – if you want children's love, just take some from her Viru and Biju.

Oh well, the monsoon is here, which means that there will be more work in the fields and less time for the diary. That's better, perhaps, than writing such thoughts.

BY THIS WILL we leave all our land, the buildings on the land and other constructions to our niece, Bijoya, and our nephew, Veerendra. They should use this estate and the money they get from selling it for their various socially useful activities. Our two daughters, Amrita and Shalmali, have the first right to any objects on the estate or in the house. Similarly, all our cash, jewellery, shares, government bonds, go to our two daughters.

We know that all the children enjoy a very close friendship, that they will sit together and decide on these matters amicably, and that there will be no bitterness; we are certain about this. We owe a huge debt of gratitude to Biju and Viru's parents, we know that we will never be able to repay them. But they have never considered the innumerable things they did for us out of affection, as favours. We, too, do not look upon this small gesture as a repayment. Our wish is to give a helping hand to their constant efforts to do good to others.

All that remains is wishing everyone well, always.

Even after the sun sets it does not cool down as much as it should. This month is bearable only if there is a good breeze at night. Otherwise, one has only to be stoical and somehow endure. Shami went to Janaki's the other day, and there's still a week for Yaju to come home. I thought of going somewhere myself, both Ranju and Ila urged me to go to them, but summer seems to have dried up my desire for any activity. To lock up the house, entrust someone with its responsibility, travel in the heat and then, after two or three weeks, just when you're feeling good, to return home – I had no wish to do all this. Anyway, the weather is bad everywhere – why go from a small fire into an inferno? So I remained here. This year Tai and Janubhayya have gone to Australia – I believe it is winter there in May and June. Isn't that strange? There was some conference to which Bhayya was invited and we literally pushed Tai into going with him. She said to me, 'You stay home but you force me to go!' I have already roamed around so much I don't feel like going anywhere. Whereas she, since she went nowhere earlier, is so deeply rooted here that it's with difficulty that she is willing to go anywhere. That's why she finds all her surroundings familiar while I, even after so many years, live here like an alien. Yaju seems to be more settled in this place than I am. Has the sense of alienation I felt in other places become part of me now?

Six o'clock and the sun hadn't set yet, but I decided to go for a long walk. Since there was no cooking to be done I sent Sonubai home, locked up the house and set out. Only open land and wilderness everywhere. There was no question of visiting anyone. I followed the road as it took me, my steps keeping pace with my thoughts. The larks would fly up suddenly from the ground and after singing a long melodious tune, settle down again. The crow-pheasant was hooting and bulbuls were delivering long lectures in loud voices. I could hear the screech of a kite – or was it an eagle? - at a distance. Actually, I wasn't thinking of anything at all, I just kept walking, looking at the imprint of my footprints in the hot dust. The usual stray thoughts crossed my mind – it's time for Mimi's letter, did Shami go to Janaki after only a week at home because of some lack in me? Was the relief I felt a sign of wicked selfishness? Whatever it is, the child went off happily. It doesn't matter whose love it was that sustained her, she grew up happily. Why have I become so anti-social? I can count the friends I have on the fingers of one hand. I'm moving away even from the family. Why? Only Yaju is mine …

At this point I looked up and saw it was late evening. I turned back and quickened my steps, thinking that when I got home exhausted I would have a bath and go to bed. I came through the ebony grove at the back of the house and opened the door. I don't like switching on lights so I bathed in the dark and came out onto the veranda to relax in the cool air. And then I saw Yaju sitting in the chair. I wanted to exclaim, 'Why didn't you call out, why are you sitting in the dark, you've given me such a fright!' when I bent down and saw that he was asleep. His exhausted face, drops of sweat near his eyebrows, his hand falling limply over the arm of the chair, the gathering darkness surrounding us and the total silence that falls for about half an hour at this time between day and night … My tears, falling on him, woke him up. I was seeing him after a month but he was not surprised to find me standing in the dark, looking at him, silently shedding tears. He got up, and drawing me close to him, sat down again and the two of us slowly fell asleep, not saying one word to each other.

When it grew bright, we went in to have our coffee. And then our exchange of news began – how come you returned early, where is Shami, has Mimi's letter arrived, when are Tai and Bhayya returning, Toshi sends his greetings, Hisayo is going to Hawaii next month, the three rows of eucalyptus on the left and the four rows of acacia in front need to be cut, and …

But what we really had to say to each other had already been said at night.

Dear Janaki,

Today is your birthday – many good wishes and many happy returns. To be honest, for years I hadn't understood the meaning of this English sentence. I used to think the idea was to say 'come back joyfully many times'. Later I understood what it meant, that it's the birthday which should return year after year. Which means: may you live long. But now it seems to me that the meaning I'd given it when I was young is the better one. Come to me joyously again and again, the way you came here last month. Speaking of wrong and beautiful meanings reminds me: when I was studying Robbie Burns in college and first learnt that 'my love is like a red, red rose' referred not to love, but to a woman, I was deeply disappointed. I turned to you sitting by me and exclaimed, 'What the hell!' And you began to laugh so much that Sir sent us out of the classroom. Your laughter was always uncontrollable. It is such a comfort to me that, even after going through so much in your life, you still have that ringing laughter. Let it keep resounding in the same way. And once again I send you the wrong good wishes: let your laughter often flow this way.

Your week here seemed like one day to me. One of us had only to speak, to respond or make a remark, for the other to immediately understand and agree; and very often both of us said the same thing at the same time. This is the way it has been for a great many years. After Tai, Dada and Janubhayya, you are the only one who has known me and seen me through the years. We may have had our disagreements but it only increased our togetherness, our bonding, the joy we take in each other's thinking. You'll say – what's all this about? But I want you to accept with pleasure these emotions which I feel like articulating and am expressing, however badly, on your birthday. Actually, there was no need to say all this explicitly. I would have left it unsaid as I have always done, telling myself that you know it all anyway. But today I suddenly thought – why do we unnecessarily take some things for granted? If we said what we felt everyone would be happy. Earlier I was the impulsive talker, you were the reserved one who made do with a small smile. But these days I've got, well, not Yaju's quality, you can call it a gift from him, of keeping things to myself; it seems to me that I'm too cautious. So I thought, I must say what I want to say. One publishes a book of poetry and says, let the reader take any poem and apply it to herself. Enough of that. So I'm writing specially to say – without feeling ashamed of being emotional – that you are very dear to me, you are almost the only link to my youth, the one friend who, throughout the years, has accepted everything and adjusted to everything. Live happily on this day and on all your birthdays – when I say birthday I mean every day, so it means all your days from now on.

Shami-Mimi, my darling beloved girls,

What can I write? And how can I say it? My mind is so full of both anger and grief that I am incapable of thinking. It's true that your grief is great; but somewhere, in some corner of my mind I have the feeling that ever since you disentangled yourselves from here and settled abroad, you were preparing yourselves, little by little, for these deaths. But we have been left defenceless. It's you who need to write grief-soothing letters to Rajni and me. And I am full of anger. I think, how could the two of them escape, leaving us so completely desolate? They gave us true love all our lives. And then, finally, to turn their backs on us like this? Like this? *What if we had done the same to them?*

Come and meet me before you go, I want to pour out my grief in your presence. Right now I am very confused, I don't know what to do, where to go; it's hard to come out of this. The only comfort is that there aren't too many days left for me to go through. 'You go ahead, I'll follow you,' this is what I am telling your mother.

You will come to see me, won't you? I've often repeated the saying: 'The mother can die but let the mavshi live,' yet I never thought of the mavshi's broken heart when I said this. And this mavshi is here. Come and comfort her.

Your
Janaki

When I heard that Toshihiko would be coming here for an entire month on his way to his son who had settled in America, I was overjoyed. Of course, he wouldn't spend the whole month with us in this little village, but a week at least! And I knew that with his Japanese trait of making the most of each moment, we would find the week full enough.

He was the only one in Japan with whom we had a good rapport, perhaps because he was the first person we met when we got there, and among all those strangers his English was the best. Later we met many others – even a couple like Yoshiyo-Hisayo of whom we were very fond – but there was nobody to equal Toshi. It could have been his trait, so unusual in Japan, of being self-critical, or his curiosity and broadmindedness which came from his having met many people during his worldwide travels, that attracted us. Whatever it was, we became friends, and our friendship was different from those we made in other places which remained only as memories. The sole reason for this was my love of letter-writing. Toshi replied, at first out of politeness and then, because he enjoyed it, he began to reply in haiku! Yaju and he would meet at least once or twice a year on account of work, and he would make a detour when travelling to visit us. But this came to an end when he retired six or seven years ago and we realised then how much we looked forward to those fleeting once-a-year visits. Toshi is a part of all our memories of Japan. At first he showed us around, explained things to us. Later, because we couldn't enjoy anything without him, he went everywhere with us. But it was with Shami that he bonded first; this, of course, because she learnt to speak fluent Japanese before we did. They would chat intimately for hours together.

Life is so strange! We often look back and regret the things we haven't done, but there are very few about which we exclaim regretfully, 'Why did I do this!' I have this kind of regret about Toshi. The opportunity was there – now I think that if I had persisted just a little Toshi would not have hesitated either. But ultimately nothing happened. That nothing happened wasn't a great loss, but what if … What would have happened? Curiosity remains unsatisfied.

That night the two of us had gone to Toshi's bar and Toshi, who was normally quite controlled, drank a great deal. At about midnight he looked at me intently, head to one side, and said, 'People of our age shouldn't go beyond platonic friendship; this is the truth.' I didn't know whether to laugh or cry, I wanted to box this stupid, wicked Toshi's ears. I opened my mouth to say something angrily but then saw such a look of pleading in his bloodshot eyes that I patted his hand affectionately and said, 'What you say is absolutely correct.' The strange thing is that I grew very fond of this stupid creature. Today when Yaju, after reading his letter, laughed and held it out to me I asked, 'Suppose I fall into his arms because we're meeting after so long, what will he do?' Just thinking of it made Yaju laugh. 'He'll try to hide behind me. He's not Dick!' That was true. And once again I felt a pang of regret for an opportunity lost.

It seems to me that till they reach their thirties and forties people simply drift along, as if their only purpose is to just go on reacting to things. No thought at all of who they are or what they want from life! Just go through the day, satisfy whatever need arises – that's it! Tai says that because of this I was a little wild until my thirties – greedy for life, for experiences and people. I used to think that to be forty was to be dead. I considered the male-female relationship to be extremely important. Part of it was rebellion against my rather orthodox parents, some of it may have been due to the individual freedoms my generation acquired so suddenly and effortlessly. But now I also think that perhaps, because of that, I turned a blind eye to my innate tendencies. It could also have been that when I realised (unconsciously) that I was a loner by nature and a reluctant giver, I turned to physical intimacy since the body can be given easily and without fuss. Easier to share that rather than one's mind and thoughts! This is why the people I feel really close to are men like Dick and Toshi, those with whom I could have had a physical relationship, but didn't – I was able to bond with them mentally, very well. Toshi and I were wise in drawing back at the last moment. How can the coarse fabric of a weekend together compare with the soft, delicate, lacy mesh we have laboriously and gently woven with four letters a year and an occasional visit? Crudity is possible only in the strong and tenacious relationship of marriage, or for the young whose resilience enables them to forget everything in a week. Toshi's words, 'people of our age can't afford to do this' were absolutely true. Now, when we meet after six years, he'll greet me in the Japanese way, from a distance, and then come closer and shake hands. And if I, very provocatively, raise his hand and hold it to my cheek, he will merely laugh a little. Only his expression will reveal the joy he really feels at seeing me; his behaviour will show nothing. And sometime during that week Yaju is bound to say, 'When Toshi meets you, it's great fun for me.'

One could write a book – no, an entire library – on this man Yaju!

Dear Mimi,

This can't be a p.s. to your mother's letter which is why it goes separately, but it's still just a small note. In a week, Shami's exams will be over. Going by her career so far, I wouldn't be surprised if she tops again. I want her to go and live with you for her further education. What do you think? Living in a hostel here and spending her vacations in this out-of-the-way village will make her very rustic. Think it over (get Vinay's opinion as well) and let us know whether it's yes or no. After that we can go into more details. Right now she says she wants to become a doctor, but since she's intelligent enough to do anything we can decide at leisure. She made us promise (and you too) that we would send her to you for a holiday as a reward for completing this phase of her education. (She's even prepared to encash the fixed deposit we had made in her name, but we have saved enough for her trip!) She will be there some time between the 25th and the 30th of April. I'll wire you the flight number. I think her short stay with you will help her decide. If you are both agreeable she can stay with you, otherwise there are many opportunities for higher education available here. Don't worry.

I'm sending a list of books I want with her, but in the meantime will you send me some simple books about how to build a log hut? I have some logs – mainly eucalyptus and acacia – of about three to three-and-a-half inches, keep that in mind.

Everything else is fine here. The entire family is collecting clothes for

Shami's Canada visit. Janubhayya even dug out some Russian fur caps of Viru's and Biju's from an old trunk! Hope they won't be necessary. Write. I'm sure you'll wire us when Shami gets there.

Your
Dada

— Wake up, Shami.
— Five minutes more, Aai.
— I think these were the first words Shami uttered when she began talking. Do you remember, Yaju?
— Of course, I do. Her first words were 'Da – da.'
— There! Daughters are always partial to their fathers.
— Freud understood this before you did.
— Ha! Understood what? There's no connection to Oedipus or Electra in this case. It's simple reasoning.
— And what is that, O Great Teacher?
— Listen, O Devotee! The mother is a creature who's just like me, she knows me through and through, therefore I must try my blandishments with my father. That's the way it is. Understood? No need to preen just because your daughters go about saying 'Dada, Dada'. Now, get up, you!
— Only five more, Aai.
— You should have had a son.
— No, thanks. A son is good for nothing At least a husband is of some use, a son is pure extravagance.
— Sour grapes.
— Not at all! I may not have had a son of my own, but I've had something to do with my sisters' and friends' sons. On the whole they're given too much importance. Just look at them - what do they have except their maleness? Only their mothers can put up with their stupid talk. When they reach adulthood they sometimes improve because of their girlfriends or wives,

or even because of their sisters. By that time, of course, their mothers scarcely see anything of them. Hey, listen, you better yell at her. Otherwise she'll be lolling in bed even after we've left.

— Shams, chams, bums, tums! If I had the time I'd write a poem on your name. Are you going to get up?

— Five minutes, Dada.

— Wah! You'll put even the honourable Rama to shame. Five minutes – not an iota of change in that promise. Come on, wake up, otherwise your mother will be furious with you first thing in the morning.

— Why make me the bogeyman? My work isn't held up because she hasn't got up! You don't have to wake up because you're scared of me.

— So, did you sleep well? Your first night here after shaking off the burden of your studies.

— Dada, that's enough. Good morning, Aai.

— Good morning, baby. Coffee?

— Aai, I want cocoa today, like when I was little.

— Hot or cold?

— In-between.

— Exactly the same! But this time I hope the two of you won't fight over its temperature, sweetness, brand, colour of the cup and saucer, how long you're going to be drinking it, etc.

— Something's got into Dada today.

— Go away, Yaju, go to your work on the well. I'll finish here and come to the fields. Watering time is at nine, isn't it?

— Dada, bring Superman out. I'm going to Anna, then to Biju's.

— Yes, sir!

— Da … *da!* Bye, see you at lunch. Aai, thanks. Shall I toast a slice for you?

— No, thanks, toast it for yourself. What jam do you want? Mavshi has sent some fresh fig jam.

— Great! Hey, where's my book?
— Shami, can I go now? The workers will have come to begin the watering, and if I don't go we'll lose our turn. Will you clear up? Just put everything in the sink, Sonubai will be here soon. Are you listening?
— Unh? Yes, yes, I'll do it. You go.
— Put that book away. You shouldn't bring books to the dining table!
— But I'm all alone, what does it matter?
— You might spill something on it.
— I'll be careful.
— Okay, okay. You've never let me have the last word before, why will you now? Now clear up properly, don't break anything.
— Don't worry, I'm not a kid any more.

— Where's Shami?
— She stayed on at Biju's for lunch.
— I thought as much. It was ten-thirty before she left for Anna's and she was going to Biju's after that. Didn't you see her?
— I was engrossed in my work.
— What are you angry about now?
— I'm not angry.
— Come on, tell me.
— She said she'd be home for lunch…
— She must be enjoying herself with Biju and the kids. What can she talk about to us? She's finished telling us her hostel stories.
— Still …
— You're very strange. When she's here you fight, and when she's not, you're unhappy.
— I don't fight, Yaju! Ever since she started school …

— Okay, maybe you don't fight, but somehow you don't really get along – not like you and Mimi.

— Mothers and daughters always bond together. Are you jealous?

— On Shami's behalf.

— She shouldn't have been born.

— Don't say that!

— No, look, it's like this – I loved her when she was a baby, she was lovely. I don't know what happened after the age of four or five, somehow every word I said, everything I did, turned out to be wrong. Finally I no longer had any energy to say anything, to correct her. Maybe this is what happens with the youngest child – my mother didn't have much to do with me, either. What there was between us came later, after I grew up. It seems to me that I'm beginning to understand things about myself, my mother, my daughters, only now. Sometimes I even think, 'Poor Shami'.

— But why? You take things too much to heart. She's doing well now, besides she has all these other parents – older sisters, brothers-in-law, brothers, mavshi, uncles …

— That's why I think things worked out better some generations back. Even if mothers weren't very maternal there was someone around who was – grandmothers, aunts, and so on. So, a woman like me who has no motherly qualities except for being able to give birth, would not be exposed.

— Good Lord! What's happened that you speak of being exposed? Ask Shami herself.

— Ask her what?

— Ask her her opinion of her mother.

— Ha! As if children think of these things.

— Then why worry?

Dear Dr Abhi,

Shami has just successfully finished her studies here. She (and Mimi too) have been talking constantly about her going to Mimi for further studies, so we have already prepared ourselves for her departure. Her father will go with her to Mumbai in a week. The two of them will meet you. Why don't you come here for a few days? After all, the car is returning and you will have company as well. We can share with you both our relief and our loneliness at being free of our daughters.

Shami left today. To put it in the language of journalism, she departed for her sister's place in Canada. My Ajji used to laugh at this. Is it a parcel? she would say. But Shami was packed off like a parcel. However much her father tries to shrug it off it hurts him that she and I don't get along, which is why he worked through Mimi to get her admitted to a university there. In spite of having resolved that I wouldn't, I cried buckets. This must have been the first time since she grew up that I held her close and hugged her tight. And I thought – I've wasted all these years. If I had made it a rule to embrace her and hold her close every night, we wouldn't have been so hostile to each other and my tongue would never have spewed so much venom. But the body is wicked; it refuses to do anything false. When you're angry, neither your hands nor your lips will cooperate.

Shami was thrilled at the idea of going abroad, especially to Canada which she has never seen, and most of all to her darling sister. She must have been fed up with her mother's tears. Nevertheless, she kissed me a few times when saying goodbye and promised she would write. She sobbed when taking leave of Superman and she'll do the same with her Dada in Mumbai. Pretending to be casual I asked her, 'Has your mother harassed you a lot?'

She shrugged and said, 'Not at all.'

— What about our fights?

To which she replied, 'I asked in school and all the girls said this is the way mothers are – boring. But you and I are a little better off. You don't lecture me about clothes, food, being tidy, or about punctuality and responsibility.'

After this I drew back. When I told Yaju he said, 'There you are! A good certificate!'

I suppose so. Anyway, I can say that even if I haven't done too well, I've got through the exams. Yaju would say I've cheated. There's that's, too.

I find it amazing: because of motherhood and my desire that my children should not lack for anything, I turned my back on many things in life, on people, on experiences. And the very children who were to make motherhood worthwhile, turned their backs on me – because I'm their mother. If I weren't, I would have got on with them beautifully, the way I do with my nephews and nieces, real ones as well as those I regard as such. Sometimes I think I should have been the father and Yaju the mother. He is tender, has the greatness not merely to forgive wrongs but to forget them, and the generosity to deny himself and satisfy others. And he does this with a smile. And my nature? Absolute justice, logical thinking, following the rules, planned orderliness – these are what I like. Like? Or crave? Ultimately I had to make the best of what came to me. In our generation, mothers provided the motherliness and fathers the fatherliness. We changed this a little, mended it and patched it up a bit here and there, but basically there was no change in the roles. Let's see what happens in the next generation. That Shami and yes, Mimi, too, is doing 'well' is a victory I think I can celebrate today.

Dear Ranju,

Yaju left for Mumbai with Shami this morning. The fact that I didn't go with them tells you a lot. Does a person get used even to parting and separation? When Mimi left I was heartbroken, but when Shami went it just seemed to be part of the process of growing up. Besides, I have no hopes at all that she will finish her studies and come back to live here. We will now meet only when she comes to see us. If, by chance, she takes up a travelling job like Mimi we might meet more often, that's all. Ultimately, Ranju, it's just the two of us. Our family and friends must have accepted the fact of Shami's going, because this time there was no discussion about whether she should or shouldn't go. Sometimes even simple calculations go wrong – that's what happened with Shami. She was born very late. She's the youngest in her generation. Nobody thought of her as anything special when she was a baby. Tai's Biju, and perhaps Viru, got that kind of attention. Even Dada's Shishir and my Mimi were not a novelty. By the time Shami was born our generation was getting bored with babies and was craving grandchildren (who started arriving only seven or eight years after Shami was born!) By the time she reached childhood and adolescence I had lost all my enthusiasm and, truth to tell, I was disappointed in her because of her stubborn and troublesome nature. The others, it seemed, took their cue from my attitude to her. When they met her they were affectionate – just a bit – but when she was away they never thought about her. Even I never understood what kind of girl she was, how could the others? Her intimacy was with Yaju and Mimi, and then with Vinay. It's right that she has now gone to her dearest sister. Mimi will be able to show off her motherliness, her big-sisterliness and Shami will get what's rare for her, a huge amount of love. You know, Ranju, last night I crept into her room. She was sleeping in her usual way, lying straight on her back. When I looked at her, I was overcome. This has been my habit from her childhood. I would look at her when she was asleep and start crying, thinking how the poor thing got nothing but scoldings all day, the entire week, through the months and years -- in fact, her whole life. I would resolve that I would talk sweetly to her, that no matter what she did or said, I would be sweet to her. But my resolve would dissolve in a few days and it would be the same all over again. I finally gave up making resolutions, but I never gave up grieving when I saw her sleeping peacefully and innocently. I held her, caressed her, even kissed her. Do you think she felt her mother's love in her sleep? A love concealed under anger and bitterness, rage and disappointment, but surfacing suddenly – I don't know. If I do this to Mimi or Yaju, they turn over in their sleep or come close and cling to me. But Shami doesn't move. Not at all. The cold wakes me up at least once at night during winter. Then I go about covering people with blankets. She would wake up only if I pulled her blanket from under her and covered her. Then she would smile and say, 'Thank you, Aai.' That's all. I remember how, when we were staying in a double-storied house, she would fall asleep in the living room downstairs. (It was such a bother for me to keep saying 'Go and sleep upstairs'.) I couldn't carry her up because she was heavy so I used to wake her up, make her climb the stairs, then put her to bed. She didn't remember any of it. In the morning she would ask me, 'How did I get here?' She's such a sound sleeper.

But yesterday, although I was standing by her silently, she woke up. Opened her eyes, saw me and said, 'Hi.' Moved a little. When I sat down beside her, for the first time in years she hugged me herself, the way she used to when she was a child. I was the one who would say, 'That's enough! After harassing me the whole day, why do you hug me at night?' Or 'Don't, Shami, it's hot.' Or, 'Why do you behave so badly, Shami?' Gradually she stopped hugging me. When she did last night, I realised how long it had been. She said, 'Never mind, Aai. I'll also earn a lot of money and come to meet you often. Okay? And Aai! You are not to sell Superman! Promise?' I just sat, nodding. It was she who comforted me. I think that in this war between parents and children, parents get exhausted, both symbolically and actually.

I sat there till she fell asleep. When I came back to bed Yaju was awake. He said, 'What was going on between mother and daughter?'

'Nothing. Goodbyes. Promises. Suggestions. What else?'

I've cried on your shoulders about Mimi and Shami, everything else I've shared with Yaju. The two of them will meet you in Mumbai. I'll visit you too in about a fortnight. Tell me when you are free, I'll come at your convenience.

Dear Toshihiko,

I've already written to you about Mimi's marriage. Now another, and in your view, a more important bit of news – about Shami's having gone to Canada. Actually, you knew Mimi only fleetingly, and though you admire her for being a bold, independent, rebellious girl the one you really love is Shami, isn't it? After Mimi settled down in Canada Shami decided she would go to her, and when Vinay and she became such good friends, she was definite about going. Yaju, too, wanted her to go there for her 'higher' education and I wasn't against it, either. (Though I didn't really agree!) And so, on the whole, she went happily. When you next go to America to meet Masanori, you must make a detour and visit Shami. She's very fond of Toshi-ojisan. Whenever we went to any attractive spot for a picnic or somewhere for dinner, I had to drag you away from your cosy chats with her if I wanted to talk to you. Remember? Once, when Yaju dropped out at the last moment the three of us went somewhere – where was it, Toshi? Was it the Katsure Detached Palace? No, children aren't allowed in there, but it was some place like that – near Kyoto. Yaju and I had quarrelled over her just the previous day. I was in a very disturbed state of mind; one glance at me told you this. And the entire day you made sure I was left to myself. I realised this at the end of the day, sunk as I was in my own sadness. When you dropped us home you said in a compassionate tone, against Japanese rules of politeness! 'She's lonely here, just as you are.' I looked quickly at Shami. She was holding your hand and looking at me. Had I spoken to her affectionately in the last ten hours, or even the last ten days? When I realised this, your sympathy pierced me more sharply than words of anger or contempt would have. I sat down, right there at the door, and drawing Shami close I managed to say, 'Why, Shami! It's you and me for each other, we're together. Neither of us is alone.' And she, responding to this new surge of love, drew her hand out of yours and putting her arms round my neck said, 'Don't cry, Aai. I'm here.'

You couldn't understand what we were saying to each other but I'm sure you knew that we were saying what needed to be said. After that, Toshi, you were very often with the two of us in our individual aloneness, because of which we could cope with a lot.

Now, when I tell you Shami has gone far away, I say – it's you and me for each other now, so come and see me. Come here on your way to meet Shami, to whom you gave one half of the heart you gave me.

Dear Shami,

How can this scrap of paper fill the huge emptiness that your parents' death has left in your life? Tears over such grief never stop flowing and that's why you shed them again and again. I won't insult your grief by writing a few words of consolation. I can only write that my tears too have not stopped flowing. Their deaths have left a huge gap in my life as well which can never be filled. But I also want to say that even if my life is now made up of such abysses, there still remain a few intact bridges – like you – which can connect them. Their support comforts me. Grow up, be sensible and scatter seeds of laughter among friends like your mother did. Remember this friend sometimes.

Your
Toshi-ojisan

We renovated the bathroom attached to Shami's room on the occasion of the house's 'birthday' and installed a shower and washbasin in it. In spite of searching a great deal we couldn't find a green basin. Shami will be angry when she comes back and sees a white one. When we were building the house we chose her favourite green for the toilet bowl in 'her' bathroom, but then ran out of money and had to use white tiles for the walls. When she complained Yaju told her, mainly to shut her up – why don't you paint a matching green flower on each tile? That was it! She got a brush and paint, and the entire holidays the brat actually painted flowers! There were still quite a few left when the walls came down and I recalled Shami carefully painting the flowers, the tip of her tongue sticking out. A great deal of the paint appeared on her nose, cheeks, ears, hands, clothes, and much of the wall had splashes 'colouring' it, but she was determined; she drew a flower on every single tile and when it was done she announced, 'My bathroom has five hundred and seventy-six tiles.' Now that she's gone it has become the guest bathroom, but when she returns she's bound to say, 'What's this! You have money now, don't you? So why didn't you get green tiles?' At which Yaju will probably give her paints and a brush again!

Janubhayya came to help with the log hut. His help actually means chattering. The man was in a good mood but because Tai would get annoyed if we kept him for lunch, I gave him some fresh garlic bread and a cup of coffee and sent him home. He had brought letters with him. One was from Ranju telling me that Sujata was getting married and would settle down in America – so many of my contemporaries' children have done that. The truth is none of us was in a position to hold on to them. Nor were our parents. We dispersed to different places, either to earn a living or because we were married, while they stayed on in their own homes until the very end. Children who go abroad seem to be lost to us. There is a huge difference between our lives, our experiences and our daily reality and theirs; that abyss can never be bridged. We write letters, we scrawl some news about our pets, about trees and flowers, about the pointless hobbies we've taken up, about family and relatives, and they write about their harsh winters, the flowering in spring, or about friends. It's all a formality. The end of a relationship begins when the umbilical cord is cut or when children are weaned. After that, it's only a question of counting the years and seeing how swiftly they go their own way. Whether it's Sujata or Mimi, whether they go to Canada, America or Australia – why, even if it's only a residential school they go to – it's just physical distancing. It's not as if there's no distance between parents and children who stay at home; the fact that there is no closeness (except for physical proximity) even when living together makes this lack of intimacy seem worse. But this distance in space entails a distancing in many ways. When it's day here, it's night there; when it's unbearably hot here it's joyous springtime there; when it's pouring with rain here (at least in Mumbai), it's summer there and people are going to beaches to swim … everything is different. They're absorbed in their lives in these new countries, but force themselves to scribble a few lines on an aerogramme.

Now it comes back to me – I had gone to a school camp and my father had given me four postcards, one for each week, with the address and even the contents written on them! All that I had to do was to drop them in the letter-box. But I brought them back. My mother grumbled and said, 'How irresponsible you are, you don't care about your parents.' At which, rubbing salt in the wound I said, 'I forgot,' and fled.

But Ranju and Sujata were very close. They had never lived apart, not even for a week, till she went abroad for her education.

I must write to her. Do others have better children or are they better mothers? I asked one or two friends this question earlier and they said, perhaps to make me feel better, 'Ultimately, it's all the same; minor differences here and there, that's all.' Ranju says she will come here this year for Divali. When she does, I must discuss this with her.

Dear Ranju,

I must admit I felt a little sad after reading your letter. Sujata went to America for further studies five or six years ago. Even at that time we told ourselves that it was very likely she would stay on. And yet … It's true that the world has shrunk, that one can come from America in just about twelve hours, that even if they had remained in this country children would hardly be living with their parents, and so on. But the 'and yet' crops up here as well. When my Mimi went we took it for granted that it would be for keeps, and we also thought this was how it should be. Do you remember how much we argued about it? Janaki and Tai said don't send her so far away so soon, she's just done her B.A., and the two of us said it's good for her to go. Good for her, good for Yaju and me, good for Shami as well, perhaps. In spite of this, when it came to it I grieved over the fact that she went, that she had to go. You saw this, you understood it. At the time I used to visit you often and we would chat about various things – just anything: new writing, books I'd read, new knitting patterns. But Mimi was constantly in my thoughts. Where did I go wrong, what should I have done, what should I not have done and what's going to happen now? You too would leave off whatever you were doing to talk to me. And then suddenly you'd say, 'Why don't you leave some things to fate?' And we would both realise that, like it or not, we knew each other's minds very well. I would laugh and say, 'I have no faith in it,' and you would reply, 'It's a great comfort to believe in it. Each person brings their own fate with them. All that we can do is lend a helping hand – or do nothing.' And then we would go and make some tea. Sujata left, not because she had to but because she wanted to, because she thought her talents would find greater opportunities there. This may lessen your sorrow a little bit – and yet …

Sujata was a great favourite of mine. Mimi sometimes thought it was because she was so good at her studies, but she's dear to me for a special reason. She's learnt the art of shaping her life the way she wants, quietly and with determination. We were, all of us, very quarrelsome. The slightest provocation and we were ready to fight. I used to think that compared to us, our daughters' generation is weak, soft, single-minded, with no thoughts of rebellion. But they're capable of getting everything they want, and among them Sujata is the best. I said to her once, 'Why do you put up with your brother's arrogance?' And she replied, 'Why should I waste my energy, mavshi? The silly fool will come to his senses some time and even if he doesn't, it's not my job to make him see sense.' This last was a dig at me. And shall I tell you the truth? I envied her that trait. I could never manage it – neither with my father nor with my husband. Our tongues were always sharpened. If we were forced to keep quiet, we sulked so that they would notice. Sujata and Mimi are really the clever ones, aren't they? I feel sorry about one more thing. Will I get to see Sujata whenever she comes? How will a mavshi living in a village get the chance when she has her parents and siblings to visit?

This is a quick note, I'll be with you very soon. We need to discuss new recipes, new knitting patterns, new writing etc., don't we? So we'll meet.

Dear Mimi,

What can I write and how do I comfort you? Even now, none of it seems real. Which is more terrible – the fact that they died, or the way they died? A hundred little things come to my mind. Her voice, her laughter, her words – I hear them so clearly; is this an illusion or is what happened an illusion? I am older than both of them. Why is it that I am the one who must write a letter like this?

I have still not recovered from the shock, and at my age I have no hope of doing so, either. But I had to write to you. You will meet me before you leave, won't you? Look after Shami – and yourself.

Your
Ranju

Dear Mimi and Shami,

We thought you would come, if not for the house's birthday then for your Dada's at least. All we got were cables. Shami's excuse is work, but what about Mimi? We've made lots of changes in the house on the occasion of its birthday; now, if you come and question us about what we've done we won't listen. This is my house and you are not allowed to interfere. Your Dada, tired of my bossiness, has extended his log hut and is making an office and workshop there. When I said Janubhayya has instigated you, he said, my banging will disturb you in this little house (especially as it has hardly any walls). You should learn from him how to give honeyed replies which have the ring of truth! The mimosa trees which we planted between the house and the lake on the house's tenth anniversary have long since grown taller than the house. So also the eucalyptus in front. The silver oak trees haven't grown much, but that they are able to survive this terrible heat is no small thing. Some of them blossomed this year – I am happy. Janubhayya's neem tree had lots of berries so he is happy. His plan is to send me every day to collect some – I only hope he doesn't start a soap factory!

It must be spring there now. Here, we are already on fire. Can we plant ourselves on you from March to June next year? Obviously, only if Janubhayya and Anna are here. Let's see. But will you come here before that? In winter?

Tell Vinay I asked about him and say that I found the two pictures he sent us very romantic. Take care. I'm sending pictures of the house.

Your
Aai

Dear Mimi,

Get me a set of tungsten-carbide-tipped concrete drills when you come and another set for wood. Buy only their own brand from the Black and Decker store – I need these for my work on the log cabin. You will love this cabin. I am building it according to the book Vinay and you sent me, thanks a lot. All is well here. I don't know whether your Star Trek will survive until next year. Now the poor thing can't see much, but fortunately his legs are okay. Anna says if a pony loses its legs, it's all over. If that happens we may have to put him to sleep; I write this so that you can prepare yourself for such an eventuality. Shami's Superman, however, is still quite sturdy. When Ashu or Samir come, I make them ride him – he can't take the weight of adults now. Our cats and dogs have proliferated so much that I can't give you news of their individual well-being by name! Your mother says we should give them away one by one. If you want to meet everyone, come soon. Sometimes I think your mother will gradually begin to give away people as well! Anyway …

Your
Dada

Today Shami became a doctor. When I read her cable I started weeping. I don't know why, but my tears just flowed. From childhood she used to say, I will become a sportsman, a doctor and a farmer. She achieved her goal of being a sportsman when she was in the university, was good enough at a tough sport like riding to win a medal, now she is a doctor. There's no chance of her becoming a farmer unless she comes back here. And since she says she will go in for research, not practice, it is even less likely that she will return. I've seen from the beginning how Shami, with grim determination, gets what she wants. Once, when she was a child, I even said to Yaju, 'She's such a little thing but she makes a woman like me yield; she's going to be great!' She had a bent towards medicine from a very young age. Whenever she came here, she *had* to visit Biju's dispensary at least once a day. Of all her siblings, she's closest to Biju – except Mimi, of course. I found – I still find – the adult Shami incomprehensible. When she was little she followed me about like a shadow. Then, at the age of five, she went to school and some link between us snapped. She was born to me late in life, my last-born, whom I had because I wanted her. I showered love on her when she was a child. Did love then dry up, like breast milk, after that? And, honestly, why did I long for a child in middle age? I can understand some of my reasons: it was the first time I had problems with Mimi and I wanted to fill up the empty space, needed to reaffirm and underline my ebbing womanhood with the dark ink of motherhood. I wanted to share with Yaju the joy of our child ... Still, all my reasons remain just that – reasons. Shami – real, live, long-faced, grave-eyed Shami with a scarcely perceptible dimple flashing in her cheeks – this Shami is now a doctor. And she's going to do research in subjects with names I can hardly pronounce. Sometimes I think that when she was about five or six I stopped listening to her and got into the habit of responding with an 'okay, okay'. Her child's mind understood this and she stopped speaking to me. I didn't really mind. But it's true that later I couldn't understand her. While working in the house I would hear her and Yaju chatting on the veranda. Her high-pitched child's voice and his gruff murmuring. I couldn't get the words but it was the background hum to family life, like an old familiar song which comes to you from afar. Sitting on the veranda I could see them at a distance returning from their walk, absorbed in talking and listening to each other. Not that she avoided talking to me, but she never specially confided in me. When she comes here in a month she will seem so grown-up, so much an equal. Why equal? Superior in knowledge, in authority. Amusing, isn't it?

Last night I must have mistakenly slept on my back so I needed Yaju's help even to get out of bed. It was impossible to do anything. All I could manage was to stand up, walk slowly and sit in a straight-backed chair … From now on, I will have to get used to this back problem, but what I feel most, even today, is anger. It is over twenty years since this pain got hold of me for the first time. It began when I bent down to pick up something without flexing my knees. And then I couldn't straighten up. I crawled to the phone, rang up a friend (Yaju was on one of his tours) and asked her to bring her car and take me to the hospital. The doctor took an Xray which hurt a lot. And then, laughing casually as if to say, 'What a fuss this woman makes of such a trifle,' he said, 'Slipped disc.' Like most doctors who think all patients are idiots he wanted to get rid of me after giving me a prescription. But I asked him, 'Why did this have to happen to me?' My words must have revealed my anger because he was surprised. He said, 'It's not unusual, it happens to a lot of people. To women more because they suffer from calcium deficiency, either in pregnancy or after delivery. It could also happen because of lifting weights or bending down, or even due to a small accident. Take these pills and you'll feel better. Try not to bend. If you have another attack, take an aspirin every two hours. Don't lift anything heavy and do these exercises every day. That's it.'

Since then, activity without pain has become non-existent. The pain may be a little less or a little more, but there's not a single hour when it is totally absent. I remember reading somewhere, 'Pain is part of a woman's fate.' I feel like adding: 'Pain and anger and fury and frustration and discontent and helplessness…' And since nobody quoted Dylan Thomas' words, 'Do not go gentle into that good night' to us, I have to include endurance as well. The few of us who rage are criticised. 'You've got to endure some pain. So what?' Of course we do, but that's not enough – we should endure it either in silence or joyfully! My mother told me once that she would howl during childbirth. Her friend, a doctor, said, 'So many women give birth, don't they suffer the pain? What's the use of screaming?' And my mother would reply, 'I feel better when I scream.' She would get angry even with her husband; but I never felt like that. I thought: this is my pain, I brought it upon myself and I must suffer it. But why a slipped disc? This stupid affliction which came upon me when I was in my forties has taken ten years of my life. Actually, ever since I was twelve or thirteen, people thought I was ten years older than my age. What does it matter now? As Tai says, when she's a hundred and ten and I'm a hundred, nobody will know the difference. But why go so far? When I was forty and she fifty people thought, if not twins we were very close in age!

It seems to me that short-statured people don't show their age early. Besides, as the doctor said, tall people have more problems with their spines. Now that people's heights are increasing, nobody says I am tall. But I'm the tallest among my contemporaries so is it a kind of impartial justice that I should have this problem? Since, in any case, I can't do anything else, I wrote some Christmas cards and letters today. This list has been shrinking the last few years. People who drop out leave an empty space and there's nobody to fill it. Except for a few intimate friends like Dick and Yoshiyo and Toshi and Robin and Ivan and Vesela, there's nobody to whom I need to write. But this is an easy and polite way of saying, 'We're alive, how are you?'

Dear Dick,

This year you will get my greeting card before any others and you will wonder, why this hurry? You once complained that my Christmas cards sometimes reached you closer to Valentine's Day – I'm trying to make up for that!

Winter has set in here as well. Not as cold as your winter, but enough to make us bring out our sweaters, coats and razais. What I like most about winter here are the birds. Much-loved messengers who come from you to us. I see a new one every day – the crested cuckoo, the swallow, the finch. The sight of the scarlet minivet makes you open your eyes in wonder, and the flock of rosy pastors gives the impression of a delicate pink sheet being unfurled. Last year, two pairs of flamingoes came to the lake – let's see if they bring some company with them this year. The other day we saw the little ones of the paradise flycatcher after years. Of course it's not a migratory bird, but you see it mostly in winter. We glimpsed a shimmer of brown in the tamarind trees, and wondering how a crow-pheasant could have flown so high, we brought out our binoculars and saw the little ones. So lovely! Yaju immediately took some pictures. I'm sending one of them (instead of ours!) to you.

Has Mincy returned from the hospital? What do the doctors say? Why don't you come here for a change? It'll be such fun! And we'll visit you next summer. Your friend is laughing at my plan, so you have to come just to prove him wrong. All the best for a happy new year, Dick. And my love, of course.

Dear Dick,

All our best wishes for a merry Christmas and a happy new year. I'm not laughing at all, in fact you must *come, I heartily endorse the invitation. Give my best to Mincy. Tell her to get well soon.*

Your
Yaju

Dear Yoshiyo and Hisayo,

Many good wishes for the new year. I'm sending pictures of the house and its surroundings. There may be one of ours among them, but from this year on we take no more pictures of ourselves. Yes, if people are as good-looking as you they should have pictures taken! But ours! Well, let's leave that. You came here when the house had just been built and you were a little disappointed at seeing the barren surroundings. That's why I am specially sending you pictures of our trees. The eucalyptus in front can almost be called a jungle, as also Janubhayya's silver oak and casuarina. The sandalwood trees, however, haven't grown much – they are scarcely about two metres high and very small in girth. And I don't know how many generations there have been of your fish which Anna let into the lake. Of the three bottlebrushes you brought, one has grown well and has flowered. What I'm trying to say is – come and see all this! Every two or three years I pester you to come and you go off to Hawaii or to Europe. Next year, start a little early and stop here on your way to Europe. March is not very hot, but if you come in July-August you will meet Shami as well – she's coming for her holidays. She's got a job at her university teaching hospital and is coming here for a break before she begins. How many years it's been since you saw her! She used to translate for all of us – now she's completely forgotten her Japanese. You'll find it strange meeting her. Children whom we've watched grow up always remain children to us. You can't imagine how Shami, whom you haven't seen for fifteen years, has grown. I don't even know what kind of work she is doing exactly, and there was a time when I threatened that I would smack her if she grumbled about reciting her multiplication tables!

Mimi was here for Divali. She comes often because of her work, so we don't feel the separation as much, but Shami's coming is rare. And if you come, too … Anyway, think about it, and be happy in the coming year.

Dear Yoshiyo,

Good wishes for the new year. I'm coming to Yokohama on work in the second week of January and will definitely meet you then. If I urge your girlfriend to come along, she'll say she won't take the trouble for just a week or two, and that too in winter. So you'll have to make do with me.

Your
Yaju

P.S. Yoshiyo, I only just learnt that this man is going to Japan – how is it possible for me to make all the arrangements and leave at such short notice? He has no problems, his bag is always packed. Anyone invites him and makes his reservations, off he goes! But it's a happy thought that at least we will meet through him. If you need anything, wire me right away, I'll send it with Yaju.

Shami, dear girl,

We were planning that this year, somehow or the other, we would meet your parents, and then this news! What can we say? All that we can do is to express our shock and sorrow, bemoan our deep distress. From where do we gather the strength to help you in your great grief? We visited them two or three years after they built the house – it's been a long time, and since then we've only had brief meetings with them in Mumbai during our stopovers. But we met in their very lively letters which gave us news of their lives and yours. We feel as if we met them just yesterday – and then today, they've got up and gone. Our only comfort is that we still have you to help us cope with such terrible losses in life. Years back, you allowed us the joy of being like your parents – now we are the only 'parents' left for you. So come to us, at least to cry your heart out.

Your
Yoshiyo and Hisayo

Men feel compassion for their wives, and in general for all women. Only sympathetic men, of course! I never thought that I would not only realise this truth, but would express it too. I took all the goodness my husband had shown me over the years for granted. Or perhaps I weighed all the nasty things he had done against the goodness and satisfied myself that they cancelled each other out; but the goodness remains. Women have many different feelings for their husbands or for the men they know: ranging from anger and rage to affection and motherliness, from scorn to respect and fear. But they never pity them. Now, am I the kind of woman anyone should pity? Yet, when I look back, it seems to me that almost all the men who came into my life felt compassion for me. I remember when Mimi was very little, my father used to carry and cuddle her and I asked him once, curiously, 'I know what a mother feels when she first sees her daughter, but what does a father feel, Baba? What did you feel when you first saw me?' He turned and looked at me over his granddaughter's head with a slightly embarrassed expression on his face. Then he smiled and said, 'I felt pity. Such a tiny mite. Not just her future, her very life and death depended on me.'

I cried on hearing his words and I'm doing the same now as I write these lines.

Do we, in spite of losing ourselves in the various twists and turnings of the road, somehow reach the right point finally? When I came here and built this house I knew what I didn't want more than what I did. Setting up house in a different part of the world every few years, then uprooting myself, snapping all the ties I had made and forming new ones, making an effort to learn a new language, discover a new place, new culture, food, environment and climate and then, with the same effort, forgetting them all – this had exhausted me, both mentally and physically. I was fed up with my constant problems with the children. Why, I even wanted to hide from Yaju's slightly accusing, sad and disillusioned eyes. My mind was so barren that the aridity I saw in this place didn't matter. Janubhayya and Tai had been with me all my life; I had nothing to hide from them, I was my own clear simple self when I was with them. I also wanted to run away from the crowds and the chaos in the city, the neighbours I had willy-nilly to accept, the insecurity in the midst of crowds, the dirt, the competition, the violence.

Then we came here. After one spell of rain we planted trees. They grew, first to knee height, then waist high; they went on growing and as they grew the aridity and barrenness in my mind receded. I began to say: *my* house, *my* groves, *my* trees, *my* well. Janubhayya said: I am planting silver oak in your grove at the borders, you can plant useless pretty trees in front of your house, but only acacia on *Yaju's* land. Tai would send messages saying: Will you send me seeds of this and that? We're short by ten kilos! And I kept saying, I won't do any work, let your Yaju do it. But I took on my share of watering, of building a wall for the well, of the girls' expenses, Janubhayya's buffalo, Mani, the cat, who appeared at our doorstep because she was scared of water – all these fell to my share. Then birds started visiting the growing trees …

When I see trees even an atheist like me becomes aware of some great limitless grace, of being specially favoured, so I think: you treat them badly, you cut them, disfigure them, starve them, but they keep giving with eternal loyalty as long as they live. What good deeds has this most wicked of all creatures, the human being, done, that trees grow on earth for them? This is how my trees grew all around me, throwing a cloak over my depression, over my sense of futility. Even Janubhayya's 'useless' trees flowered gloriously: gulmohar, laburnum (Ranju's haldi-kumkum), cassia, jacaranda, the champak, the flame of the forest, the coral tree, Shami's namesake, Shalmali, the silk-cotton, the night queen, the jasmine – and one special spice garden.

I kept saying, 'I'll do it, I'll do it,' and finally I did it in Dick's memory. He had said he was coming and was ready to come, but fell ill just as he was leaving. And then I started working to get over my disappointment, my enormous depression. Once, when we were in Holland, I had gone with Dick to an old fort. While other tourists were admiring a variety of old things – weapons, clothes, pictures – he took me behind the fort saying, 'I'll show you something interesting.' Yaju, seeing the two of us slipping away, opened his eyes wide; Dick winked at him and took me out. I could see nothing special; small beds with paths running through them, a few small bushes bearing neither flowers nor fruit. I was confused and looking at him, thought – was Yaju right? Dick's eyes were closed, he said, 'Take a deep breath.' I did and, yes, there was a fragrance, sharp and fresh, something you could barely catch. My mind, floating on that fragrance, gradually made its way home. Slowly I separated them and said: basil, marjoram, southernwood, ajwain, coriander, rosemary, lemon grass, mint! Dick was ecstatic. He opened his eyes, pulled me towards him and, laughing, kissed me repeatedly. Still laughing, we sat down and began carefully identifying each plant in the beds. He said, 'I was sure you would identify them, you come from the land of spices. That's why I didn't use any aftershave today. You never use perfume, anyway. Now tell me, can any scent in a bottle or any flower be more delightful than this?' I wanted Dick to come and see, no, sniff my 'Dick's spice garden'. Since his illness has affected his eyesight, I send him at least one leaf from my spice garden in every letter and he sends me another in his reply, something we don't easily get in this warm climate – like rosemary.

Because I'm so crazy about fragrances, Tai made a graft of a tree someone had brought from France – the fragrant babul – and gave it to me for my birthday. It's just outside my window and has an unsurpassed wafting fragrance. Now I ask myself, why did we roam around so much? But our wanderings did bring us some rare gifts – like Dick's rosemary: rosemary for remembrance. Remember Hamlet?

It seems, then, that we didn't lose ourselves in the turns and twists. Things happened as they should – that arid isolation as well as this abundant sense of belonging. This is the right place, and a safe one, in which to store the accumulated memories of our travels. And the strange thing is that our daughters who haven't lived here much and who have now settled in other continents – for them, too, this is home. Today I got letters from both of them wishing this home a happy birthday.

Today Viru brought Ashu and Samir here so that they could learn to ride the pony. It was a short holiday with 'Mau-ajji' for them, and a good way of passing time for me. But teaching them to ride is Yaju's and Anna's job. I have never been able to get friendly with this creature called a horse. I learnt to like all animals, even cows, bulls and buffaloes, but not horses and ponies. I had made a kind of truce with Mimi and Shami's Superman and Star Trek – I would stand at a distance and offer them a carrot, that was all! Cats and dogs are, of course, rulers in our home. And so many other animals have visited us at different times – squirrels, rabbits, ducks, bulbuls, even a mongoose. Why I can't bond with horses, I don't know. Today Ashutosh patted Superman and quickly climbed on to him, just the way Shami used to. Samir was frightened and so, therefore, was Star Trek. Once frightened, Samir refused to get up on Superman either, and while Ashu was able to ride around the house within an hour, Samir wouldn't allow Yaju let go of the reins. I was amused. Looking at them, you think it is Ashutosh who is shy and stays in the background. Samir is a chatterbox, rash and mischievous. But it's exactly the opposite when it comes to sport. I'm always amazed at the differences in children. These two are the offspring of a brother and sister, born within a week or two of each other; they've grown up together, in their own houses as well as in ours. But how different they are! Okay, they are cousins, but even real siblings are not alike. Look at us, Tai and me, Biju and Viru, Mimi and Shami …

Watching Ashu, I was reminded of Shami. She sat on a pony for the first time in a park in Mumbai, insisted on it. She enjoyed seeing the other children go past, laughing, bouncing, swaying, trotting. But when she sat on the pony herself, she realised how strange and different this animal was from her and she began to howl. Nevertheless, when I tried to get her off the horse she clung to its mane. She went round twice, still wailing loudly. It was the same performance the next day. It took her a week to get used to it. By this time she had become an object of curiosity to the ponywallas, the children and their parents. 'She cries so much, why does this little one still persist?' they would say. 'Ask her,' I would reply. But when we came here and Anna brought Superman, he became her most beloved companion. Anna got him because he was docile, clever and slightly clumsy, but in her opinion he had absolutely no faults. Today when Ashu sat on him, he was happy. Maybe – who knows? – Superman, too, remembered Shami.

February is over but I haven't written anything in my diary. One look at it tells me why – this one is different from the earlier ones, all alike, all attractive. But this one I can't look at, find it hard to touch ... it's like the black-bordered letter which came on the twelfth of November. How quickly one registers anything that is unwelcome and inauspicious! The moment I saw that letter, I thought: Dick! I felt like a chameleon which has been injured by the stones thrown at it by callous children. Yaju wasn't with me either, to open the letter, read it and offer me his compassion and loving support. Slowly, I put out a trembling hand. My tears began to flow even before I opened the letter. There was no need to read Dick's name in glossy black print. Mincy had died a year earlier. My condolence letter now had to be written to myself. Later, when I was sending out Christmas cards to friends, I was angry – why are you still alive? And me, as well, who is sending you good wishes for the new year? What use am I in a world that has lost Dick?

Today Anna came from Mumbai, brought us sea fish because it's so rare. Treating this novelty with ceremony, I decided to follow a special Yugoslavian recipe and garnish it with a few rosemary leaves. I wasn't really thinking of anything, just sitting on the shady side of the beds in the spice garden, plucking tiny sprigs from the rosemary bush, when suddenly the fragrance splintered the numbness of my mind. Rosemary for remembrance. How did Yaju, watering the watermelons two groves away, hear my soundless cry of grief and rage, with his ears as well as in his mind? And why, in spite of having felt such knife-stabbing grief earlier, why was I still not used to it? All of us, even I, keep saying that our sensations get blunted as we grow older making it easier for us to bear things. Why, then, does grief remain razor-sharp? Is it because it peels off our skins one by one, so that when death comes we have reached the point of not wanting to live any more?

I met Dick five years ago. I find it hard to write the words – *for the last time*. Photographs of that time show that his hair was soft and pure white, both his almost-blind eyes an ashen grey. His skinny and tall frame was like a long bamboo staff, bent in the same way as the bamboo, but his near-snub nose looked as if it had been sharpened. When I look at that picture now, I am surprised. This was not the Dick I saw! For me, he was still golden Dick, the first truly golden man I had ever seen – in real life, I mean, not in the movies. Other so-called blondes are yellow, or the colour of coir or just plain dull. I used to think – what kind of blondes are these? They look like dark people whose colour has faded. Dick was really golden, like twelve or fourteen carat gold, a little light, as if mixed with silver. His hair, his lashes, his eyebrows, the hair on his body – everything was such a rare golden colour, you would think that after this man was created he had been sprinkled with gold dust mixed with silver. He had come to Schipol airport to receive me. Taking advantage of the fact that I was in Europe I put shyness aside and hugged him tightly. I realised then with a shock that I could feel every bone in his body. But after that I saw only the earlier golden Dick, not the silvery one of this picture. Is it surprising that with Dick's silver and gold reduced to dust, I see only darkness?

From now on my diaries will be these black diaries. And rosemary – for remembering, for forgetting, for shedding tears.

People were surprised when we decided to live in a place so far from almost everywhere. They asked me whether, after having lived in so many countries and Indian cities, I would be happy in this sparsely populated quiet village. To which I replied, 'As far as I'm concerned, I can be happy anywhere.' The truth is, it is easier for me to get on with myself than with other people. It's like this: by the age of fifty a person realises how worthless he or she is – or, at least, they should; living then becomes possible only if you can ignore your own worthlessness, or if you carefully avoid thinking about it. Similarly, telling yourself constantly and in various different ways how useless others are, is a good way of ignoring your own worthlessness, but this means you gradually begin to dislike other people's company. The problem is if you don't associate with others you don't see their faults, either – though, of course, magazines and newspapers very successfully make up for this lack. They say that I loved company as a child and girl, that I had a host of friends with whom I enjoyed myself. This, obviously, is my siblings' account. Of that host of friends I don't remember a single one. When people tried to remind me about themselves, except for thinking, 'I knew this person once,' they didn't matter to me at all. It's possible that at one time I had enjoyed collecting friends, but people rarely accept the fact that either they, or their friends, can change. For quite a number of years now I have given up making new friends and don't bother to keep up with old ones, either. But nobody has acknowledged this change in me.

On the other hand, there are times when I wonder: do people really change? Or do natural traits finally emerge from the many superficially imposed roles and various concealed layers? I was the youngest in my family and there was quite a gap between my siblings and me. I was born when my parents were already middle-aged and so very early on, I got used to being a loner – a habit which I suppose, was driven underground for some years by the mating instinct. Is it possible that it is making its presence felt again? If not, why is it that I am quite happy not to open my mouth for days together, except to eat and drink? There was a time I used to talk a lot. Now it's an effort for me tell Yaju about something interesting that I've read. He'll read it himself some time, what's there to tell?

It was Janubhayya's seventy-fifth birthday today and Tai had invited everyone to lunch – the two of us, Dada and Vahini, Biju, Viru, their spouses and the grandchildren came together after a very long time. But the surprising thing is that Janubhayya himself was not in the mood. Biju even asked him, 'Dada, aren't you feeling well?' Which made it worse. Very rudely he replied, 'Why don't you forget your profession at least for one day?' Everybody was quite upset after that and we soon dispersed. When we returned home we sat on the veranda, brandy glasses in hand, feeling depressed. We understood Bhayya's rudeness which is why we found it hard to say anything. 'In another ten years we will be where Bhayya is now': these unspoken words gave rise to a fear which tasted bitter in our mouths.

Years ago Bhayya used to say, seventy is a good age to go. When he was forty he said it emphatically; when he was fifty he said it with a small smile; in his sixties he said it feebly. And now in his seventies, he doesn't say it at all! And today? Bhayya's hair, his beard, his moustache, even his eyebrows are pure white. He looks like a saint. Only his eyes are sparkling and mischievous. Without his beard and moustache he would have looked like an infant. He has an innocent smile even when he's cracking an indecent joke. People would sometimes say to me, 'Your brother-in-law is very handsome,' which surprised me. I mean, Janubhayya is Janubhayya, Dada is Dada, Baba was Baba; can they also be handsome? But now I see that Janubhayya is good-looking, the way very simple and innocent people are – glowing with goodness. Even though his features are irregular, his laughter lights up your mind – that's how beautiful he is. I'm sure he has never wronged anyone. Tai is my favourite person in the family, but after knowing him for fifty years I wonder who's closer to me – Tai or Bhayya? Just look at this – nobody takes anything that Bhayya says amiss. They say Janu is Janu, and leave it at that. But if Dada or I were to say the same thing it would become a big issue. The point is everyone knows Janubhayya has no desire to hurt anyone, that he doesn't want to show off, he just says whatever comes into his mind – that's all! If we upbraid him saying, 'How could you say such a silly thing!' he smiles and readily apologises.

I was very young when Tai got married; it was the most important event in my twelve-year old life. When I first saw Janubhayya I thought he was a strange creature. Everything about him, including his name, was odd. Shrujan Bhatnagar. The tallest man I had ever seen. With dark and curly hair. Narrow, slanting Chinese eyes. A snub nose, lips so thin they scarcely seemed to exist. And above them, a brownish moustache. What a combination! He had a Bengali father and a Maharashtrian mother which is why his Marathi was indescribable. And because he had done his high school and college in America, even his English was hard to understand. I had only to look at his face to laugh. And then he would laugh as well, showing a gap where one of his front teeth had fallen out. Of course I fell in love with him. A few years later, full of guilt about my feelings, I confessed them tearfully to Tai and she laughed and said, 'Silly girl! Everyone falls in love with an older brother-in-law!' I was so relieved.

Janubhayya was his parents' only child. They died a few years after his marriage, following which he considered our family his own. We, of course, were already his family but he bonded with scores of others! So many people come to this deserted place of ours because of Bhayya. It never occurred to us that something was troubling him. But today, in the midst of everyone – his grown children, his son and daughter-in-law – he looked as if he had withered and shrunk. Seemed withdrawn. We didn't know what to say, what to do. We came back and sat for a long time in the dark. When I looked at Yaju I noticed that his beard and moustache too were white enough to be seen in the dark, and unconsciously I passed my hand over my hair.

Christmas is just a month away, I must bring out the list of cards tomorrow.

The milkman's son let go of the buffalo and she went berserk, stampeding straight to the log hut. Only after smashing into it did Madam stop and come under control. The wall on the side of the well was almost completely destroyed. Once she was secured the milkman, the watchman and the servants got into a huge argument about who was at fault. Still quarrelling, they came to tell us about it. I was so stunned that it never occurred to me to blame or scold anyone. I rushed out with them, hoping there wasn't too much damage. The walls facing the house were still standing – but when I turned the corner, there was only a gaping hole. Yaju was standing there, staring at it. His tools, his revolving chair, drafting table, many of his books – all buried under the logs. Cups, saucers and glasses had fallen from the shelf on the still-intact wall and were lying smashed to pieces. The biscuit tin was on the ground, biscuits strewn all over the room. Suddenly aware of my presence, Yaju turned and I saw the tears in his beard. He made no attempt to wipe them. Leaning against that half-broken wall, silent, I began to cry, too. Seeing me like this, everybody was silenced and walked away slowly. The round table and four chairs on the other side stood exactly as before – as if waiting for the four of us to sit and have our coffee. There was a pad and pencil on the table for Janubhayya to make quick sketches and demonstrate how something should be done. I went in and quietly began picking up the pieces, but Yaju went back to the fields. It was almost twelve by the time I finished clearing up. When the servants left for their lunch I went home. Yaju was sitting outside, flipping through a magazine. He said, 'Sit down. I'll get our lunch and some beer.'

I said, 'Why beer today?'

He smiled and replied, 'To celebrate the fact that one more shackle has fallen off. Let's celebrate "days of losing" now, instead of birthdays.'

He's right. Once a transfer is imminent we know we have to start clearing up soon. How did I, who am such an old hand at transfers and departures, forget this? First we dispose of things we don't need, so that finally what's left is just one vessel to boil water in, coffee and tea tins, and two cups. Tolstoy said two feet of land is enough for a man to be buried in, but we'll be cremated so even one foot is plenty for us. Janubhayya had said, 'What! Waste all this manure? No way! We should be buried and a tree planted over us. So choose. Mine will be a banyan.'

I must make my choice before we get to the point of two cups, and tea and coffee tins.

I've started thinking I should stop writing my diary now. Why keep moaning in it day after day? This has gone wrong, that has gone wrong – was anyone responsible for what happened today? Maybe, as Yaju says, the surprising thing is that it didn't happen earlier. A goat got into the garden at night, ate up my entire spice garden, trampled on the tomatoes and chillies below the kitchen window and finished off our greens. Did someone let it in knowing that the watchman was on leave for four days? What use is it now looking for a reason? What's lost is lost. The only thing it didn't eat is the ajwain, but the pot is broken. My southernwood, marjoram, mint, coriander and turmeric – all gone. How much of it was I using, anyway? I would crush a leaf once in a while and inhale, that was all! The lemon grass for tea is still there, isn't that enough? Why worry about the garden when Dick has gone? With this gone only memories remain – like rosemary. We drove the goat out and let it go. If Janubhayya had been around he would have had it tethered, and when its owner turned up he would have asked for damages. Would have said, 'I'll take it to the butcher and slaughter it, I won't let it go …' I merely drove it out and closed the gate. When Sonubai came she said, 'Ararara! All the tomatoes are lying in the mud, shall I see if there are some good ones left?' And I said, 'Take them home for yourself.'

Yaju didn't go into the fields that evening, he tried to put the spice garden in order. He propped up the few plants that were still alive and watered them. I sat on the veranda watching him. When he came in the strong odour of the plants clung to his hands and clothes. I thought of Dick who, forty years ago, hadn't used aftershave so that I could smell their fragrance. I closed my eyes and inhaled deeply Yaju's earthy smell.

Tomorrow morning, should I get the workers to cut fresh planks from the acacias ? Yaju has repaired my spice garden; I will set up his log hut again. I was always impulsive and he was always controlled. Now that I have become such an introvert, is it surprising that he has become almost totally silent? He stood passing his hand over the broken wall as if he was stroking Bhayya's body. And it was not he, but I, who shed tears all over again. We had had to put our own sorrow aside and comfort Biju, Viru and the grandchildren when the jeep accident happened. I shed those tears very often now, making sure Yaju doesn't see me. But Yaju, who avoids the log hut, weeps within himself. I will go there now and put the logs together. It doesn't matter how badly I do it, one day I will take Yaju there and say, 'Look, fix it, this log doesn't sit right.' He may come. He may tell himself, 'This hut is now hers, not mine and Bhayya's', the same way that I have told myself, 'The spice garden is now Yaju's, not Dick's and mine.'

It's forty years since my mother's death and thirty years since my father's. I have no vivid 'final' memories of my mother. There are others – of her anger, her approval (more of her anger, though) her discussions, her concern which could always be felt, and her affection which occasionally emerged from her detached intelligence. It happened rarely and when it did, it shook you. And above all, her uniqueness and the enormous awe she inspired for her scholarship – so much so that it was almost a burden. On the other hand, what I remember of my father is his cheerfulness, his loud voice, his fondness for jokes and a childlike nature which made it possible for him to mingle easily with children. And his final short illness. When I recall this, regret joins grief. Should we have done something more? Should we have struggled to keep him alive, disregarding his own wishes? Should we have, somehow, postponed his death? And would anything we did or did not do have deferred it? Helpless, I shed tears even now. And there's anguish in my grief. Can there be any grief as pure as this primal grief over the death of a parent? Then I think, we will be making a gift of this grief to Mimi and Shami when we go. Our deaths will churn up so much more in them – anguish, regret, anger. What should we do? Should we go on living one futile day after another just to protect them? Agonising over family members and intimate friends who have gone? Or should we go as we have decided – together? Neither one leaving the other behind. Like Tai and Bhayya. I want to go. What should we do? There was a time when I was afraid of death; although, when I thought about it seriously, my past and present life seemed more futile than dying. I got goose pimples when I thought of condemned prisoners who know with certainty when and at what time they will die. But no longer. Of course I'm still scared, but I have learnt to think of only one step at a time. Crushing some sleeping pills – that's one. Dissolving them in a glass of brandy is next. Sitting together on the veranda, glasses in our hands, chatting affectionately with each other the while – this is one more. Then the consequence of the first three: a numbness slowly spreading from our limbs to the rest of the body … Many years back Yaju scolded me, saying I was so preoccupied with past and future happenings that I lost sight of the 'now'. Since then I have trained my mind to dwell only on the 'now'. My whole life lies behind me and nothing is likely to happen in the future; therefore it is easy to live only for the 'now'.

A very funny thing happened recently which brought this home to me sharply. I hadn't really taken note of the way the town nearby had grown – first a school, then a college. A few days back some boys from the college came to meet us, they must have been curious to see these old fogies living near their town. They seemed well-behaved – drank tea, saw the house and the fields and asked Yaju some questions about farming. And then they began nudging one another, making signs as if to say, 'You ask them.' Finally one of them plucked up his courage and asked in a childlike way, 'Having lived like this for so many years, you must have learnt something about life. What have you learnt?'

Yaju and I looked at each other and began laughing. I wanted to say, 'You don't learn anything about life just by living.' But I felt sorry for the boys, I thought I must say something that they can put down in their notebooks. I had just watered the methi beds and climbed the stairs with some difficulty. I said with a smile, 'If you keep going, one step after another, you are sure to reach somewhere, in time.'

They wrote this down quickly and went away smiling. I thought, 'This is not a bad philosophy for life: keep walking and the road will come to an end; as one moment overtakes another, the day ends; as days follow days, death approaches. And if you write page after page, the diary comes to an end …'

Mimi and Shami, our darling daughters,

We know that our dying in this way will fill you with anger before you begin to grieve, because the one who commits suicide is free but those left behind are held guilty, by themselves as well as by others. Therefore this letter.

If we were to tell you now that the two of you brought pure happiness into our lives, it would be hypocrisy; all of us know that's not true. And so we say that you brought animation into our lives, ups and downs, fun, liveliness, problems, disappointments, sorrow, laughter, happiness, hopes – it has been a fountain of excitement, and for this we are truly grateful.

Why have we taken this decision? In the last three or four years we have lost many friends, and Tai and Bhayya's death in an accident last year was the last blow, almost impossible to bear. We began to feel that grief and agony had become the ruling emotions of our lives. It seemed futile to live a life in which each day would be just like the previous one. We realised, with increasing certainty, that there were very few people left who would understand what we were saying and share our memories. We also realised that we only had each other and that if one went, it would be too much for the other to bear. You will grieve – it's true. But we comfort ourselves with the thought that all of us have to sorrow over a parent's death at some time or other.

The four of us have loved one another very much, we have done so much for one another, we have given a lot and taken a lot from each other – this is what matters most.

Up to now this letter has been from both of us, these next few lines are only Aai's; you'll know as soon as you read them.

You will ask – why did we decide to do this today? It isn't anyone's birthday or an anniversary: of the house, or someone's wedding, or of a death. What's so special about November 17? Why did we decide, 'no more' today? The answer is so simple that you will laugh. Today our newspaper's annual subscription comes to an end and we find it tiresome to think of renewing it and reading the irrelevant, meaningless news for one more year. My darlings, be happy, take care of yourselves, but don't be so careful that experiences turn away from you, frightened by the fences you put up.

All our blessings.

Your
Aai & Dada

Afterword

It was some time in the 1970s that I first came across the name Gauri Deshpande in a Writers' Workshop anthology of poetry by women. Having read little contemporary poetry by Indians, I felt a sense of startled surprise on going through this volume – for the first time I was hearing authentic Indian women's voices in English. It seemed to me, too, that these poets were using English with greater felicity than the novelists, but above all, was the feeling that they were saying what I would have said, were saying what I needed to hear. Some of the poems stayed with me, one of them being Gauri Deshpande's 'Migraine'. In time I read more of her poems; I had realised by then that she was the daughter of Iravati Karve, whose book *Yuganta* had made me – and many other readers, I'm sure – look at the characters in the *Mahabharata* in a completely different light.

My first meeting with Gauri took place many years later when I was on a visit to Pune. Vidya Bal, the editor of *Miloon Saryajani*, a magazine dedicated to women's voices and issues, invited me to meet a few of her friends. The only one I can remember today is Gauri, not only because of her striking personality, but because of a remark she made. Someone brought up the question of who we write for, and Gauri very laconically said, 'I write for Vidyatai and Shripu'. (Shripu was her publisher, S.P. Bhagwat, of Mauj Prakashan.) There was some laughter at this, but when I came to know Gauri a little better, I realised that she meant it – she wrote for these two individuals, not for a magazine or a publishing house.

The best way of knowing a writer is through her work and *Miloon Saryajani*, to which Gauri contributed regularly, gave me a chance to read her writing on a variety of subjects, both light and serious. I also read in the now defunct *Indian Review of Books* an article of hers in English, which I consider one of the finest I have ever come across on translation. In this piece Gauri wrote about her translation of Richard Burton's *Arabian Nights* into Marathi which, she very matter-of-factly said, she did to earn some money. However, translating the sixteen volumes was an enormous job and took her ten years to complete. Most of the translation was done when she was out of India, with nothing but a dictionary to help her. The article was, characteristically, a very personal piece – original, probing, provocative. Totally shorn of pedantry and theories, it spoke directly from her hands-on experience of translation. She wrote about the discoveries she made during the process – such as how even a man like Richard Burton, despite his great familiarity with and sympathy for the Arab world, brought a subtle orientalism into his translation, exoticising the world of the stories. She recognised how anti-women the stories really are and remarked, 'How alienated from women a culture must be to base one of its oral texts on the fact of a woman's sex-crazed infidelity.' There are also some gems about language in this piece, one very discerning discovery of hers being that Richard Burton had toned down the language to suit the susceptibilities of Victorian England. This was something she decided to correct, as during her childhood she had heard the women in her family using explicit Marathi words for bodily functions. But she adds, 'While I was not looking, Marathi had travelled towards Victorian English', and many outraged readers complained about the use of some words in her translation! One of her most important observations about this process is that the translator, for a deeper understanding of the text, must speak from 'inside' it. To speak from the outside, she says, is to look at it as a strange world, needing explanation and a display of curiosities. With such an understanding it is not surprising that Gauri disliked the trend of English writing by Indians, which she thought was written from the outside, for the western reader. This was her charge against *The God of Small Things*, made in an article which began by saying, 'I know I will be accused of jealousy for saying these things, nevertheless . . .'

By this time I had read some of Gauri's novels as well. Hearing from me that it was difficult to get Marathi books in Bangalore, she sent me a packet of her novels signed in her large distinctive hand. For a reader who hasn't read much of a particular literature, to read a single writer is to have no context in which to place her. In spite of this handicap, I found Gauri's novels unusual; there was much in them that was totally unexpected. For one thing, they were novellas rather than novels, short, but densely packed. And intense. The language was difficult and cryptic, at times almost coded. (It was reassuring to learn later that people whose Marathi was much better than mine also found her language difficult.) Her protagonists were intelligent, rational, thinking women whose ideas about themselves and about relationships were out of the ordinary and to whom, very often, friendships mattered as much as families. What struck me as strange was that her characters were not the kind of people one expected to find in a Marathi novel. At least I, with my limited knowledge and preconceived views about literatures in the languages, did not. Not only because there were foreigners called Ivan and Dmitri in them, but because of their lifestyles. These people travelled easily and often, had lived abroad, had friends in different countries. Above all, they were unconventional – cosmopolitan and with very liberal views. All this offered to the reader in the most chaste Marathi.

However, anyone with a knowledge of the family Gauri came from (which most Marathi readers would have) would not be surprised at the kind of people and the world that Gauri created. She herself had a unique background. Her mother, Iravati, was not the only distinguished person in the family.

Gauri's grandfather, Dhondo Keshav Karve (more commonly known as Maharshi Karve), the great social reformer who was given the Bharat Ratna when he reached the age of a hundred, was a crusader who worked for the education of girls. (My mother remembered him coming to their house in Pune, pleading for the girls in their family to be sent to his school.) He opened a school for them which later became the SNDT University, and a home for widows; he propagated widow remarriage, and married a widow himself after the death of his first wife. His eldest son, Raghunath, a teacher of mathematics like his father, took up the cause of family planning and opened the first birth control clinic in India in 1921. His views were so radical that he believed that not only should women be liberated from constant pregnancies and too many children, they should be able to enjoy sex. What was more, he and his wife decided not to have any children themselves. It's not surprising that the couple were reviled and ostracised. Gauri's mother, Iravati, had done her masters in sociology from Pune University and received her doctorate in anthropology from Berlin in 1930; for years she worked in Deccan College, Pune. Gauri's father, Dinkar, had a doctorate from Leipzig and was professor of chemistry and later Principal of Fergusson College. Her sister, Jai Nimbkar, was also a writer in English. And the list goes on. Apart from their academic distinctions, many in the family had married people from different countries, communities, religions and languages.

Gauri was shaped by this background; her life was not the usual life of a young woman of those times. As she herself said, she inhabited two worlds, the conservative world of Pune and a more cosmopolitan and liberal one. She also possessed two languages, English and Marathi, and was comfortably bilingual and equally creative in both. More unusual is the fact that she wrote in exactly the same way in either one. In *The Lackadaisical Sweeper*, her collection of short stories in English, it is hard to tell which story is translated and which was originally in English. Her journey through the two languages is also interesting: she began by writing poetry in English, wrote short stories in both languages, and later wrote poetry in Marathi as well; but her novels she wrote only in Marathi. Meenakshi Mukherjee, in an article on Gauri written after her death, commended her for moving away from English at the very time that Indian English writing was getting known internationally. Not many writers, she says, would swim against the stream in this way. I wonder if it was that simple. In fact, it seems surprising to me that people can attribute a writer's use of any language to 'choice'. (In India, writers are spoken of disapprovingly if they have 'chosen' English, and approvingly if they 'choose' to write in their mother tongue.) As Gauri said in a letter to her publisher, it is the material that chooses the form, the material which decides whether the work will be a short story or a novel. So, too, with language. I don't think a writer consciously chooses – the work, whatever it is, comes to her in a particular language. Meenakshi Mukherjee considers an emotional article written by Gauri on her mother after her death as a turning point, when she shifted from English to Marathi and from poetry to prose. But Gauri herself in an interview with Gouri Salvi, said that she began writing in Marathi when she was away from home and hungered for the language. It is also possible that her early poetry in English was an unconscious way of seeking the anonymity she might never have had if she had written in Marathi. The truth may well be all of these and yet none of them; the fact remains that Gauri was truly bilingual in a way few writers are, and this was part of her family legacy.

Yet the family's distinction and fame could be a burden as well. She felt it especially when her first marriage ended in divorce; for someone with the name Karve, there was no place to hide. Not that Gauri wished to hide; she was a forthright woman, open and candid about everything, including her personal life. In her biographical note in the Writers' Workshop anthology she clearly stated, 'Married twice, two children from the first marriage, one child from the second.' This at a time when divorce was still a dirty word. I imagine what hurt Gauri was that her mother did not approve of her walking out of her marriage, and that she didn't support her when she did. Gauri makes the surprising statement (surprising to all those who have read *Yuganta*) that her mother really was a traditional woman, wasn't a feminist at all. All her research and writing proceeded from her intelligence, not from her concern about women's issues. Undoubtedly, Gauri had very conflicting feelings about her mother, admired her greatly for her intellect and achievements yet felt her lacking as a mother – 'She was not the hugging-cuddling type,' she wrote in a piece for *Miloon Saryajani*. More importantly Gauri constantly measured herself against her mother and found herself wanting. This is evident in some of her letters to her publisher, Shripu Bhagwat. Edited and published by Vidya Bal in a festschrift on Gauri after her death the letters are, I would think, unique in the history of publisher-writer relationships. They date from the time she was a bubbly student in the US to when she was close to death. There is almost nothing she did not write about: writers and literature, family and friends, her own writing, analysing it as if Shripu was a sounding board; she wrote on women's writing, on love and life and death, and more. In one letter she speaks of her sense of inadequacy, something any daughter of Iru's (her mother) was bound to feel. While her mother was successful on so many fronts, Gauri felt herself lacking in every area. Writing about the tradition in her family of doing good for others, she regretted that she had done nothing but write -- and of what use was writing to the world?

Such sentiments are surprising because the impression Gauri gave was that of great self-confidence. And vitality. It is possible that such thinking was brought on by loneliness, which was even greater when she lived in countries where English wasn't spoken. In the last years of her life she was tired of travelling, longed to be home, yet reluctant to live away from her husband. Later, there was her illness, a result of alcoholism, and the depression that accompanied it. 'She was not at peace with herself,' a niece said after her death in 2003.

Gauri's sense of failure about her work, her feeling that her writing was being ignored, that she was being left behind, was grounded in some realities. She was criticised for writing about privileged people – it was said that all her protagonists were women like herself. This is a problem in a country where literary criticism embraces factors like caste and poverty; writing 'about' the privileged classes by a writer from that class is generally regarded as being less significant. In one of her letters to Shripu she said that the women she wrote about were educated, they had enough to eat and a roof over their heads – did it matter whether they received love and respect from the men they chose, whether their children lived or died? Is it surprising then that she was brushed aside, left behind? In addition, there was her sense of being marginalised, being ignored by the mainstream, a problem that many women writers of her (and my) generation have faced. Yet in reply to a letter from Bhagwat in which he praised her writing, she said she was embarrassed by the praise. What surprised her was that 'you men' do not mention women's contribution to Marathi literature in any of your public speeches – apart from 'the usual triumvirate of Vibhavari, Iravati and Durga – with Kamal Desai* as an also-ran'. All the rest, she said are put in brackets or footnotes, 'though Nemade and Chitre don't do even that'.

---

*Vibhavari Shirurkar, Iravati Karve and Durga Bhagwat, eminent writers of the early twentieth century.

Perhaps the fact that she lived abroad a great deal because of her husband's job made her unaware of how her work was regarded at home. When for a brief while she decided to stay back in India (they had built a home in Vinchurni, in rural Maharashtra, close to Phaltan where her sister lived) and resume teaching in Pune University, it was said that a great number of students chose English because of her. By the time of her death she had carved out a unique place for herself in Marathi literature. The list of her publications is enough to put her fears that she had achieved nothing to rest. She had written poetry in both English and Marathi, novels in Marathi, a large number of articles in both languages, and had translated plays, novels and non-fiction from Marathi to English, and English to Marathi (she translated a story of mine when commissioned by the editor of a Divali special issue; I treasure that translation); her translations alone would grant her a special status in the world of literature. There are not many creative writers who are willing to devote so much time to translation, indeed to translate at all, because translation requires a total submerging of one's own ego.

In 2003 Vidya Bal published a special issue of *Miloon Saryajani*, dedicated entirely to Gauri. At the launch the hall was packed with people – Gauri's family and friends, readers and admirers. She had been a controversial person, a controversial writer; but in that room I felt a kind of buzz, as if everyone had come not to mourn her death but to celebrate her life. And I realised that this crowd of readers had an emotional bonding with her, something she would never have had if she had written only in English.

Yet, to write in any one Indian language is to be read primarily by readers of that language only. It seems unfair that readers should have no access to other literatures, that writers can seldom reach readers outside their language areas. One reason I translated *Nirgathi* (the Marathi title of *Deliverance*) was because I wanted to share it with readers who don't read Marathi. It is a strikingly uncommon novel, short but powerful, densely packed with emotions, ideas and tangled family relationships and a very unusual style of narration. It is a novel about mothers and daughters, and about motherhood; Gauri has cut through all the cant about motherhood and given us its torments, its anguish.

Although I had heard that *Nirgathi* is based on Gauri's own family and experiences, I read it only as a novel. When I got in touch with Gauri's family for permission to translate it however, her daughter Urmila (who lives in the US), bluntly told me, 'My sister and I are the two daughters in *Nirgathi*.' She admitted that the novel had disturbed her, that she had felt betrayed, and that she had written something in response because she felt the other point of view needed to be presented – 'My way', she said 'of offering another possibility.' Perhaps it was our correspondence and her reading of my translation that prodded her into completing what became her novel, *A Pack of Lies,* published in 2009.

To embark on any work, whether translation or one's own writing, is like the beginning of an adventure – you never know what awaits you. The emergence of Gauri's daughter as a published writer has been an unexpected and satisfying offshoot of my translation of her mother's novel. I am sure Gauri would have been enormously pleased herself. I also think that two women, mother and daughter, offering two different perspectives on their relationship and experience is a unique literary phenomenon.

As for the question: autobiography or fiction? Urmila, from her new point of view as a writer says, 'Fiction is fiction, no matter how closely it is based on reality.' I completely agree. Even if Gauri did use her own experiences as a launching pad, I am sure the novel eventually took on a life of its own and the characters grew beyond the people she had based them on.

It has been a great pleasure to translate *Nirgathi* and make it accessible to non-Marathi readers. I must thank Gauri's family for trusting me with it and Umi, especially, for responding to all my queries without hesitation. Unlike Gauri, I started this work with not one, but three dictionaries; despite them, I would have been lost without the help of my brother-in-law, Dr Avinash Desai, who gave me the living meanings of some words, something dictionaries can never do. I owe a great deal to Vidya Bal's memorial volume on Gauri, *Katha Gaurichi,* which gave me access to much information on her and her letters to her publisher. Thanks finally to Ritu Menon, for being so much more than a publisher.

SHASHI DESHPANDE
Bangalore
August 2010

An Interview with Gauri Deshpande

Gauri, in the contemporary Marathi literary world your name stands out for a certain boldness of thought, a breaking of many barriers, which few have managed. Where does the courage for this come from?

I know that people wonder about my life because the style and content of my writing give the impression of an unusual upbringing. But it was unusual only to a small extent. You see, my family was full of thinkers, intellectuals, social reformers… My mother was Iravati Karve and my father was Dinkarrao Karve, my grandfather, Maharshi Karve and Ra Dho (Raghunath Dhondo) Karve, my uncle. And to these I can add the Paranjpyes – Wrangler, Shakuntala and Sai who were my second family. But at another level, I've had an extremely ordinary 'Puneri' (of Pune) middle-class upbringing.

So what were the unusual elements in your life?

The one thing about my family which was radically different from most other middle-class Maharashtrian families of that time, was that my mother went out and worked and more than that, made a name for herself in the academic world of men. Perhaps what was even more unusual was that she had total independence, and that my father supported her completely in whatever she did. He never ever thought that her primary responsibility was the home and children. I still remember the number of times my father would dress us, plait our hair and send us to school because my mother was away at work. He was an extraordinary man for his generation.

He'd done his doctorate in chemistry from Leipzig and yet was satisfied with being a professor at Pune's Fergusson College and then later, its Principal. But he was determined that my mother be allowed to move ahead in her career. He was aware of her extraordinary capacity as a thinker and he recognised her urge to go ahead. My mother did her graduation and post-graduation after she got married, and then it was my father who insisted that she go to Berlin to study anthropology further. But otherwise our life was much like that of any other middle-class Maharashtrian family … For instance, the extended family was very close-knit, so festivals were spent together with uncles and aunts and cousins; and many of our activities were done as a collective. Very strangely, there was a strong element of conservatism too! Girls were not allowed to stay out late, and marriage for girls was a must at a certain age. So at one level these things were very traditional.

That's very unusual for a family of such progressive thinkers …
Yes, that's quite true. It was a unique combination of a fairly traditional and normal family atmosphere, within which individuals were unusual and non-conformist for that age. Many of them had travelled the world, studied in the best universities abroad … perhaps this liberal, western education shaped the men's attitudes towards women, this looking at women as equals? And their uniqueness was that they did not have these attitudes at the intellectual level only, but actually lived them in their daily life.

One of the most important things I learned from my parents was that if you are convinced about taking a certain step, doing or not doing a certain thing was right. And as long as you are not committing a crime, you must go ahead. But then you must also be prepared to face all the consequences of upholding your convictions. Much of this I have brought to my writings …

I wonder if this is what many other Marathi women writers mean when they say that you 'write like a man'. That you have not really experienced the kind of inhibitions that they have, the kind of restraints that families or society put on them. In that sense, you are not the typical Marathi woman writer. Would you agree with this?

(Smiles.) Yes, in large part. If we look at censorship as something imposed from outside, I have not experienced it, but at times I have felt discriminated against because I am a woman. However, I must say there was no discrimination or censorship that prevented me from writing exactly what I wanted to write, or from publishing it. Nor has there been self-censorship on account of what family or friends or society will say. Now that could be because I always felt that my family was by my side, supporting every word that I wrote.

And yet when it comes to internalising some kinds of censorship, there's a very ironic twist here to my life as a writer. As I said earlier, my parents and most of my older relatives, despite being extraordinarily liberal in so many ways, were almost Victorian when it came to matters of sexuality or man-woman relationships. Would you believe it, despite the intellectual atmosphere at home and my mother's own extremely modern education, she never told us girls about menstruation! So that when I first got my periods I was shocked at what was happening to me. All she told me was that this would happen every month . . . nothing more than that. It was my married sister who told me what it was all about.

So there definitely was this conservatism, and in a strange way I may just have internalised some amount of it in the content and style of my writing. I have always felt that sex is a very private experience and very different for different individuals, so I've always asked myself: who am I to solidify in words, feelings that are experienced wordlessly? And all the descriptions I ever read sound so clichéd anyway – the same old tropes and symbols! Rivers/oceans/drowning, or earth/

leaves/blossoms. I didn't want to get into that. What I did want to get into was sexual mores and their double standards, and such things. And no amount of censorship would have stopped me – not that anyone tried!

And where did this drive to redefine sexual ethics – which you constantly do in your writing – come from?

For this, credit goes to my uncle, Ra Dho.* I was influenced by much of his writing which was unique for that time. He argued that sex is just another appetite that each one of us has to appease in whatever way we can, and society uses many ways to regulate and channel this powerful drive. There may be those who feel that the price to be paid for satisfying this hunger is too high in terms of mental, emotional and even physical health, and they may not go looking for appeasement outside the framework sanctioned by society. It goes without saying that this framework is nothing short of the bars of a gaol where women are concerned. Our present society has almost denied sexual desire to women – they are merely objects through the use of which men satisfy their hunger – with the result that women who seek sexual satisfaction in ways not sanctioned by society are condemned as 'immoral'.

What I learned from Ra Dho's writings is that one should not link *lainghigata* (sexuality) and *naitikata* (morality) – the one really has nothing to do with the other.

**Ra Dho (son of Maharshi Karve) is well-known for his pioneering work in the field of family planning in Maharashtra. He started a magazine called* Samaj Swasthya *(social health) in which he wrote thought-provoking articles on sex, sexuality, the use of condoms, polygamy, etc. He was a radical thinker and social reformer in every sense of the terms, and a man far ahead of his times.*

At what stage in your life as a writer did these influences start emerging in your work?

Now you may not believe this, but let me tell you anyway. Ra Dho died when I was 12, and all his published and unpublished works were brought to Pune and kept in our house. Since I was so young I was forbidden from reading his books but, of course, I did sneakily read them. My readers will easily find echoes of his beliefs in my texts.

My women characters, like one in a recent short story who has an 'unacceptable' relationship, have the guts to ask: 'Why do you call me immoral? Have I sent children into prostitution? Have I bribed? Have I murdered?' In our society, these 'immoralities' are tolerated but not women's sexual desires. But while questioning the societal restraints that have been placed on women's sexuality, I did not mean to give undue importance to sex, nor did I want to go into graphic descriptions of the sexual act. After all, there is far more to a woman-man relationship than sex, and I always wanted to write about the complexity of human relationships.

But do you, in fact, write 'like a man'?

On the contrary, I would say that I write very much like a woman! In fact, I have understood life and its multiple experiences *because* I am a woman. I would hate to be a man … I think they are useless beings. I have often said publicly that I despise the entire breed of men … except my men friends and my husbands who are acceptable because I've had some hand in straightening them out! So how can I ever write like a man?

No, obviously, what they were referring to was a certain fearlessness in your writing …

Well, yes, that may be correct. I'm – to use that lovely Bombay word – completely *bindas* (derived from *bindhaast*, meaning totally fearless) when I write.

Has this affected your daughters?
In one way or another, I think my unconventionality *has* affected them. For instance, I lived in this very middle class colony in Bombay in the early '70s and I lived there with a male friend. There was endless gossip about me and I'm sure my daughter was asked nasty questions, but brave girl that she had learnt to be, she fielded them by herself – at times with fists! But my family always supported me. I was able to live according to my convictions a little more easily because of that support. As a family we've all been pushing various boundaries in our lives, so maybe this pushing comes easily to me in my writing as well.

When my daughter Urmila and her friend, Ashish, decided to get married they came and told me and my husband's and my spontaneous reaction was: 'Why on earth do you want to get *married*?' But they said they wanted children and Urmila felt that society was still not ready for children born to single mothers. Even so I told her that if they did decide to have children without getting married we would support them wholeheartedly, but ultimately the decision was hers. These have been the kinds of attitudes that I was brought up with. And I think – but I may be wrong – that I have not imposed on myself the kind of self-censorship that most women writers would have to battle with.

There exists another kind of unconscious self-censorship inherent in one's class, caste and gender that may be unavoidable and from which I may also suffer, but that is for my readers to decide.

You were very young when you first got married, weren't you?
That strange conservatism of my parents decreed that daughters had to be married by a certain age. My sister's marriage was 'arranged' when she was 21. When I told them that I was 'seriously' interested in this man, they immediately

got busy, met his parents and arranged the marriage. I was 19! How 'serious' is one at that age? There was some mitigating factors – my mother was ill with a life-threatening disease; they were both uneasy about, and too old and traditional to deal with my sexuality, whatever. Of course, the marriage was a disaster.

It's not that I was humiliated or harassed in any way but I always felt boxed in, I could not push at any boundaries. And I felt these restrictions very intensely, as the very young do. So we finally got divorced. I had had two children by then. After the divorce Urmila lived with me and Mithoo with my husband. The intention was to get the girls together every holiday, but that didn't work out as my ex-husband moved to Canada when he remarried. So Mithoo has not really been a part of my family. Among other things she feels hurt that Urmila and Saheli who are half-sisters have a close relationship, while she is a stranger to both. Painful as it has all been, I have written about these experiences in my stories too – after all, creative writing finds its material where it can, even in one's own life!

Did you yourself grow up in your mother's shadow, as it were? What did it mean, being the daughter of Iravati Karve, renowned anthropologist, thinker, writer ...

Yes, I did grow up in her shadow. I realised that especially after I began writing . . . but then her writing was completely different. And there is more to it than that. For example, take her *Yuganta* which is so rightly celebrated. I have a lot of problems with *Yuganta* . . . I feel, for instance, that she has completely ignored the validity – and non-validity – of legends, epics, in contemporary life. I believe that Iravati was a traditionalist, not a feminist. Whatever she achieved in her professional life as an anthropologist and whatever she wrote was done brilliantly, but it was all a part of her own evolution, not connected to the problems of women. My mother's worldview was different from mine – maybe it was the generation gap? I don't know. So you see, it was more than dealing with being in her shadow …

A common reaction to many of your stories is that you write about ideal situations for women, that the reality is far removed from how you portray it …

Yes, I have heard this too, but I do not write about ideal people and situations in my books. If you read my writing carefully, you'll see that it is not so. I do feel that in this day and age a woman can find the strength to say: this is what I am and this is what I believe in and this is what I will do, come what may. Once she shows this strength then society, too, shows her respect. It may not have been so easy a couple of generations ago, but it can be done today and not only in my class of society. Of course, I write about the class that I am familiar with, the educated middle class, but what my stories try to say is that such women can exist and they can bring about these so-called 'ideal' situations if they set their minds to it and have the courage of their convictions.

The women I portray in my writings have often been labelled irresponsible, but this is not so. When I present a woman as an independent, determined individual she has logically thought through the consequences of all the actions she decides to take, and she tries to find the strength to face those consequences. She knows she will have to get ahead and evolve by cutting off relationships with those who do not think as she does, and who therefore hamper her own development; this is a price she is prepared to pay.

To get back to constraints in writing, would you say that your entire career as a writer has been untouched by any form of externally imposed censorship?

Actually, there *has* been one kind of censorship, if you can call it that, which has perturbed me endlessly and that is the trivialising of women's writing or, as happens in our Marathi literary world, simply ignoring it. Nobody mentions contemporary women writers, it's as if we don't exist. In a fairly important essay on contemporary Marathi novelists (written by a man, of course!) would you believe that there were literally two lines, and that too as a footnote, which said that in the '70s Shanta Gokhale and I wrote a book each? And that was it! That is all that was said in the entire essay! What happened to all those contemporary women writers who have been writing for decades now? Look at the amount of research and comment on men's writings, but nobody talks about ours.

There is simply no critical appreciation of women's writing. For instance, I've experimented a bit with form, I've taken the *rondeau* format from western music and used this in one of my novels. I don't know of any other Marathi writer who has done this, and no critic has noticed it – or if he has noticed it he feels it does not even merit a mention, leave alone appreciation.

Do you think they simply dismiss women's writing because, according to them, the world that women write about – the domestic, the personal world – is not important enough?

That's actually a fallacy. A lot of women are writing about both worlds now and then, look at the men – they totally exclude the domestic world as if it never existed! If you see the works of the early Marathi women poets like Muktabai, Bahenabai, Janabai, you realise how remarkable and astute their observations were, and yet they had never ventured out of their worlds. But the world they spoke about is the world which will last for a million years.

What is your readers' response to your characters?

Men say I do not portray men as they are. The response to that, of course, is that men do not portray women as they are

– so we're quits! About my portrayal of women they are silent or think I am portraying myself!

And what is women's response to your portrayal of male characters?
I have a curious problem here. Many of them have said to me that they find the male characters in my stories to be very understanding, almost ideal human beings! I feel very sad when I hear this because if this is how they feel, then their definition of who an 'understanding' person is very shallow. With a very rare exception or two, most of the men characters I've described in my stories are typical middle class Indian men who are what I call 'negative', in that they do *not* beat their wives, they do *not* harass them, they are *not* drunkards, etc. – their virtue is all 'negative'. What do they do 'positively'? Nobody asks that question, and I feel so sorry that women have such low levels of expectation that they are only looking for negative qualifications in the men in their lives. Where is their expectation of love, respect, ability to communicate, to interact with them and with the world? Don't these things matter in their relationships?

To move on to another topic. You are a bilingual writer, some of your writing is done in Marathi and some in English. How do you decide what to write in which language? Do you find it easier to handle certain genres in a certain language, or to express a certain kind of thought in one language and another kind in another language?
It's very strange. I've often thought about this myself, and in all honesty even I don't understand why I write some things in English and other things in Marathi! Till just over a year ago, I wrote my poetry only in English and my novels only in Marathi. I wrote short stories in both languages. I have just started writing poetry in Marathi and it has been flowing so easily. It's something I simply cannot explain. My husband's

job has taken us to various ship-building nations – most of them non-English speaking, like Spain, Holland, China, Japan, Yugoslavia, Russia, Italy, Germany. One does manage to pick up a smattering of words and phrases in different languages to get by, but what I have observed is that it's in these situations, in these lands, that I most yearn to write in Marathi, read Marathi, speak Marathi. I miss the language so much! So most of the writing I've done while staying in these non-English speaking countries has been in Marathi.

Have you ever thought of writing a full-length novel? And if not, why not?

I think there is one thing lacking, if I can call it that, in my writing I never investigate the past of the women that I write about – I never probe or go into what it was in their early lives that made them what they are. The stories of all my women protagonists begin in their 20s. I don't deal with their lives before that. Perhaps this is why I don't write novels. Perhaps I'd be bored with their antecedents or the multiplicity of characters and I think if I get bored just writing this novel, imagine the state of utter boredom my poor readers would have to go through! So I've been happy with the short story and the short novel. Perhaps I'm just lazy!

Gauri, what is it that keeps pushing you to write?

Pushpa Bhave, literary critic, once said about my writing: 'Gauri's characters do not live next door to us. They are imaginary characters and should be read as just that.' True at one level, but you know all writers write about situations they are familiar with. In my own life I have come across strong women, but I also know that too many women, throughout their lives, continue to struggle with questions like: 'Will I ever meet a man who will understand and appreciate me? Why am I not valued? Why am I not respected?' And then, in despair, they just continue to live a life of continuous compromise – as I have described in one of my books – 'with demolished self-esteem, shoulders drooping, neck pulled in, tortoise-like'. I write about women who scorn such compromise. I want women to know that they *can*.

There are many urges in a woman's life in terms of her relationships at various stages of her life – the sexual urge, the urge for motherhood, later, the urge for companionship – but I feel that women have to pay a huge price for all of these. Men don't. My attempt, through much of my writing, has been to ask: why can we not demand an equal man-woman relationship? Women are not inferior physically, mentally or emotionally, why should we continue to have unbalanced relationships? Just because it's convenient for this society as we know it to keep women from realising their full potential? I try to deal with these issues in my work and my women protagonists are always trying to hold their own in this unequal world. Making one's own space, in whatever situation one finds oneself, is a matter of life and death for us.

Interviewed by Gouri Salvi